A WOUND THAT WILL NOT HEAL

A WOUND THAT WILL NOT HEAL

A CARTER McCOY NOVEL

ERIC BEETNER

LEVEL BEST BOOKS

Praise for the Carter McCoy Novels

Praise for *The Last Few Miles Of Road*

"Beetner breaks out with *The Last Few Miles of Road*, a perfectly crafted crime story. Terminally ill vigilante Carter McCoy is the hero we've been waiting for, finding purpose and connection in his waning days as he weighs the moral burden of taking justice into his own hands. I absolutely loved it."—**Laura McHugh**, award-winning author of *What's Done in Darkness*

"Beetner has spun another notable tale here. Noir at its best."—**David Swinson**, author of *The Second Girl* and *Sweet Thing*

"Featuring an anti-hero straight out of an Elmore Leonard novel, *The Last Few Miles of Road* is a twisty-turny country noir with a heart of gold. Beetner conjures up a cast of memorably heartbreaking characters, featuring an angel of death killer trying to make the world better, one hit at a time, and a femme fatale in the guise of a desperate teenager, eager to live a better life than the one she was dealt. Carter and Bree are the 21st-century Bonnie and Clyde, and I can't wait to see what's next for them!"—**Halley Sutton**, *USA Today* bestselling author of *The Hurricane Blonde*

"*The Last Few Miles of Road* is a scintillating tale of sorrow and salvation. In aging, tortured Carter McCoy, Eric Beetner has crafted one of the least likely thriller heroes you've read about, but I dare you not to root for him!"—**Joseph Reid**, bestselling author of the Seth Walker series

"In *The Last Few Miles of Road*, Eric Beetner puts a welcome new spin on the revenge thriller by giving his elderly avenger an extra motivation: He only has months to live. Beetner also digs deeper into the unexpected consequences of going vigilante, resulting in a thriller that leavens the suspense with nuance and humanity."—**Steve Hockensmith**, author of the Holmes On The Range series

Praise for *Real Bad, Real Soon*

"I loved it. A really well-crafted story with a fresh plot and characters that stick with you. It's been a while since I've read a book that was this much fun and had this much heart."—**Jon McGoran**, author of *The Price of Everything*

"*Real Bad, Real Soon* is a thrilling, hard-hitting crime novel that doesn't pull punches. Do not miss this."—**Best Thriller Books**

"*Real Bad, Real Soon* is a first-rate thriller and a powerful hit of noir darkness, ideal for every crime fiction addict."—**Deborah J. Ledford**, author of *Havoc*

ONE

At first, Bree thought it was an earthquake. The pounding on the door wasn't a call to be let in; it was a panicked warning. The one-bedroom apartment she and Katie rented since arriving in California sat on the corner of a two-story stucco horseshoe shape with open-air hallways and palm trees growing high above the roof line from the interior courtyard. They didn't get solicitors or uninvited guests. Certainly nobody hammering on the door in fear at eight in the morning like this.

Bree checked the peephole and didn't see anyone for a moment. Maybe a prank? Kids from the building banging and then running away? She heard the low whimper of someone crying and then noticed a flicker of movement down low.

"Marta?"

Bree opened the door. Their neighbor from the end of the floor, twelve-year-old Marta, stood there with tears rolling over her blushed cheeks.

"They took her," she said.

"Who?" Bree asked.

"Isla."

Katie came from the bedroom to see what the commotion was. "What's going on?"

"It's Marta," Bree said, pushing the door wide and ushering in the girl. "She says her sister is missing."

Katie bent down to Marta's level and put her hands on the girl's shoulders. "Aw, what do you mean? She's not home?"

"They took her. The ICE. Men in a van. They took Isla."

Bree and Katie locked eyes as Marta fell into Katie's arms, crying against her chest. It had been happening more and more. Men rounding up anyone who looked Latino, anyone speaking with an accent. Men who identified as ICE agents, but with no proof or warrants for arrest. They pulled people off the streets, out of their jobs, from courthouses.

And it wasn't unusual to get U.S. citizens caught up in the mess. Isla and her kid sister were citizens, born in California to immigrant parents. Parents who were rarely home because they were out looking for work or taking seasonal jobs that kept them away for weeks at a time.

Isla, at nineteen, had already finished two years of community college and, in addition to classes, took on all the responsibilities of both her parents when they were gone. Bree and Katie happily babysat when Isla needed a hand. Marta knew she could trust the girls, even though they'd only lived there a few months now.

The quiet coastal town hadn't been the plan when they escaped Minnesota. They'd always talked about L.A. But when they hit the ocean after a slow and steady drive West, instead of turning South, they decided to stop for a few days to rest and celebrate achieving their goal of making it to California. For both Bree and Katie, it had seemed like such a long shot. If it weren't for the help of the old man who fell into their lives, they'd still be miserable in the cold, possibly in jail. Maybe dead. The beach town, situated midway down the coast between San Francisco and Los Angeles, was all they ever wanted or needed.

Since they arrived, life had been good. Slow and unremarkable, which was quite the change from the blood-stained finish to their time in the Midwest.

They knew what it was like to reach out for help, and now here was this little girl coming to them. How could they say no?

Bree brought Marta a glass of water. "Explain what happened."

After a drink and a moment to calm down, Marta explained. A co-worker of Isla's had come to tell her that Isla and three other people had been taken. Two men in a van stopped them, asked for proof of citizenship, and then drove them away even after she had produced a valid California driver's license.

Marta didn't know a whole lot of details, and she had no idea where Isla was taken. She had nowhere else to turn, no one to save her sister.

This was beyond their depth to help. Bree gave Katie a helpless look while Marta continued to bury her face in Katie's sweatshirt. Katie could only shake her head and mouth, "I don't know." But Bree thought of the old man. Of Carter McCoy.

They'd been forbidden to call, or to reach out directly. They didn't know if it was safe. Katie's father and Bree's brother were dead; a direct connection between them could be made if Carter was ever confirmed as the common link between the murders. It wasn't easy, but they had remained cut off from Katie's mom, who she loved, and Bree's mom, who she loathed. But until they heard otherwise, they respected the silence.

Bree went old school. She sat and wrote a letter after they gave Marta some food, and she fell asleep on the couch. She could overnight it, get it there probably faster than Carter would check his email anyway.

Maybe Carter would know how to help. Maybe he wouldn't, but they knew for certain they couldn't save a missing girl on their own. If Isla had been taken by legitimate ICE agents, then maybe nothing could be done outside the courts. But if what Isla's co-worker had said was true, that these were just bounty hunters looking to cash in on the government's hunger for feeding the deportation machine. Then all of this was illegal. And there had been too many reports of U.S. citizens being detained, even deported, despite their legal status. And still more reports of men using the cover of a government job to snatch women off the streets and do anything they wanted with them.

They got Marta some food, found the address of her school, and called to say she wouldn't be in that day. They reassured Marta that she could stay with them as long as she needed to. Katie put on the TV and sat with Marta on the couch while Bree went out to the post office.

With no other options, Bree put the letter in the mail in an overnight envelope. Maybe Carter would ignore them. Maybe Carter wasn't even still alive. But it was worth a shot.

Carter read the letter for a third time. Inside the familiar smells of Mesa Grande with Ivana nearby, worrying her hands into knots, his mind went to the West Coast. He'd thought of Bree and Katie often since they left, but they were brief moments when he let himself indulge in the hopeful idea of how well they must be doing and how much he had helped start the next chapter in their lives. In his mind, he had saved them from danger. With this letter, he knew that he could never insulate them from the world of evil outside if it was determined to get in.

Bad men circle like wolves, no matter what state you were in. It's why the world needs hunters.

He set the letter down on the counter. "So, when do we leave?"

Deena, the worker from Carter's friend Ken's nursing home, was confused. "Wait, where are you going?"

"Sorry," Carter said. "We'll have to postpone lunch. Some people need my help. Old friends of mine."

"My daughter," Ivana said quietly.

"Oh my God," Deena said. "Of course. You do what you need to."

Carter thanked her for her understanding, and she called an Uber. Ivana started talking about flights to California.

"We should drive," he said. "Leave right now. I can't leave Chester behind for that long, plus we'll need a car when we get there. And the cost of plane tickets."

Ivana considered it, but her mind was too scattered to argue. "Are you sure?"

"It'll take longer, but it would take at least a day to figure out boarding for Chester and then renting a car and everything. If we go right now and switch off driving, we can make it in two days."

"I guess," she said. "Let me pack some food."

"I'll go close up the house and pack a few things. Meet you back here."

"Okay."

Carter spoke to Chester on the drive home. He let a stream of consciousness out, justifying his driving halfway across the country to help with something he had no idea if he could help with.

"I always told them if they needed me, no matter what, no matter when, that I'd be there. Well, here it is. This is the call."

Chester yawned. He didn't need any convincing.

Carter took a certain pride in being asked to help. After they left, after the blood had been cleaned up and the threat of arrest had died with Brian DeFore, Carter often wondered if he had done the girls any good, really. Had he complicated their lives more than he'd helped them?

If they were asking for his help again, he must have done something right.

He packed a small bag, threw the remaining cans of Chester's dog food in a bag, closed all the windows except for a small opening in the living room. A bird that had sought refuge from the cold had moved in and refused to leave. He didn't want to trap it inside if he didn't know how long he'd be gone. He set the small suitcase by the door and lifted his coat from the rack. The bird came out of hiding with a chirp. It landed on the back of the couch.

"I don't think you much care, but I'll be gone for a while. I won't be around to set out any crumbs for you, or water. You're on your own."

He fit a Minnesota Twins baseball cap onto his head and hung his coat over his elbow. The bird flew to the windowsill, turned back and chirped once more, then ducked out the small opening and out into the crisp air.

Carter watched him fly away, wondering if he knew something Carter didn't.

The doors locked, windows closed, he stood in the yard looking back at the house. Taking any kind of trip with his limited days, he had to consider that it could be the last time he'd ever see his house again. If he were stepping into danger, or if his body simply wouldn't last long enough for him to return, he tried to imprint the sight of the house on his brain in the event it became his last.

As if he could ever forget the house where he and Ava lived for so long. The house where Audrey had been born and lived until she moved away. The house he couldn't bear to leave, even when his whole life began to evaporate around him, leaving him in a dry desert with this land his only oasis.

He hefted Chester into the truck. "I wonder if you ever went on any road trips before we met," he said. Chester shook his head, spraying drool around the front seat. "Just try not to gas us out, okay, bud? It's gonna be a long drive."

He knew Ivana would bring food for Chester, too. The cheap cans of wet food Carter bought gave the old dog fierce gas, but Ivana's plates of meat and beans made him happy and gassy in equal measure.

Before he went anywhere, Carter had a stop to make.

* * *

She packed way too much, but wasn't sure any of it was useful. Ivana was only half focused, her mind already in California, embracing her daughter who had been forced into radio silence by the actions they'd taken against her father, Ivana's husband.

Time had scarred over the hurt, but left them both with a darkness that clung to them like a shadow.

She put an eclectic mix of clothing, too many shoes, toiletries, and a set of rosary beads she hadn't seen in years in her suitcase.

Now that they were coming, she knew Carter would understand if she broke the embargo on phone calls. She dialed her daughter and was crying before she even answered.

They talked over each other in Spanish, tears from both ends of the line. Ivana got a few scant details about what had happened since the letter, but she reassured them that she and Carter were coming and that they would do whatever they could to get Isla back safely. What that entailed, she had no clue, but that was Carter's job. Her job was to embrace her daughter and squeeze her to the point of breathlessness.

For the first time since Eddie's death, it truly felt like a new start.

* * *

It had just passed one o'clock when he pulled into the cemetery. He considered for a moment leaving Chester in the truck, but he knew the dog liked walking the rows of headstones, and he knew Ava and Audrey would have liked having him come by. He lowered Chester to the ground and let him lead the way.

Carter brushed a few brown leaves from the stones and stood back to look at them both.

"I've got to go for a while. Not sure when I'll be back. Not sure *if* I'll be back, if I'm honest. These days, well, who the hell knows? Someone's asking for my help, though. Bree and Katie, and some girl they know who needs some help. I guess I got the vote. Gonna drive there. California. It's been a hell of a long time since I took a road trip. That time we took Audrey to Door County, maybe. Or Mt. Rushmore."

Chester lay down across both graves. Carter pushed his hands into his pockets.

"If I don't come back…"

He didn't finish. Neither of the two most important women in his life had a chance to say a proper goodbye. He didn't know what one sounded like. No words could say enough.

"Love you." He blew a kiss to each stone, then ran his fingers over their names before touching the blank stone where his name would be carved someday soon.

She was exhausted, but couldn't sleep. The lights never went out. Isla leaned back against the wall of the room. The cell? She didn't know what to call it. A converted garage with a steel door, windows covered and blacked out, built to keep people in at all costs.

There was a switch for the overhead lights, but no one dared turn them off. Not Isla, not the older couple clinging to each other in the corner, not the three others who came in with Isla. Nightmares happened in the dark. They needed to be ready for the doors to open, for this all to be explained. So the lights stayed on.

The three she came in with, two men and one woman, spoke solely in Spanish, keeping mostly to themselves. Isla had only been at her job a few weeks and hadn't made friends yet. She worked in the remote office at a construction site. No hard labor for her, but also no mingling with the workers outside her mobile home office. Isla knew some at the job site were illegal, some with fake documents, and some openly undocumented and getting paid in cash under the table, but she noticed none of the business owners or floor managers ever got arrested in these raids. The white ones.

The older couple who were there when they arrived seemed to not know English at all. They held on to each other like they were clinging to the edge of a high cliff wall.

Isla spoke her parents' native tongue, but she'd picked it up by osmosis. Her parents had encouraged her and Marta to only speak English. To learn it without an accent. Her mom and dad had come here as illegals, but she and Marta were born here. Anchor babies, the news liked to call them. All

Isla knew was they were Americans. She'd never seen the hills of Honduras, where her parents came from. Never tasted the food, sweat in the humidity, listened to the insects in the jungle. California had been home her whole life.

And now here she was, taken from a job site for looking like something she was not. Commanded from the Oval Office and Supreme Court approved.

The converted garage had a utility sink, so they had water. It had a toilet in the back corner, but the door had no lock. The room had been stripped nearly bare. No boxes of Christmas decorations, no unused exercise equipment like most garages Isla had seen. A custom-built holding area. A backyard, DIY prison cell.

At the sound of the locks being turned, everyone shied away and moved slowly away from the door. With a heavy metal thunk of the steel clasp, the door yawned open. The two men who'd abducted them stood in the narrow gap. A wiry man was there with a gun in one hand, ready for trouble. A more solid man with a tightly cropped beard stood behind him with three McDonald's bags.

"Dinner," he said. He tossed the bags on the ground, letting them spill. As quick as it had opened, the door slammed shut again.

The bags sat for a full minute with nobody moving. Then, one of the two younger men scooted forward, got to his knees, and reached for the bags. He tipped out a small pile of paper-wrapped burgers, and he passed them out to the group. A few mumbled *Gracias* were said.

Isla leaned back against the wall, unwrapped her sad cheeseburger, and ate.

She'd eaten her share of fast food burgers and what passed for Mexican food at any number of big chain taco shops. Money had always been tight. She'd grown up determined not to end up picking fruit like her parents, and they were even more determined to have a better future for their girls. Her job as office manager on a construction site had been a good one. But when the site was raided, she'd made the mistake of coming out of the trailer and asking to see ID from the two men claiming to be ICE. For her impertinence, she'd been stuffed in the back of the van with three others and driven away.

She never saw the IDs.

She knew this wasn't the last stop.

"What do you think?" she asked anyone who might answer. "Where do we go from here?"

A mixture of shrugs and head shakes.

"I have a birth certificate, if they'd let me get to it. They can't deport us, can they?"

"They can do what they want," one of the men said. So he could speak English. "Fuckers been grabbing people off the streets for months."

"Yeah," said the woman next to him. "And they don't come back."

They were resigned to it. The old couple in the corner could see only fear ahead. Whatever came next, it would be bad. Isla knew she wouldn't give in, not with the law on her side. But laws meant a little bit less each day, it appeared.

Her parents had taught her patience, if nothing else. She could wait. She could watch for an opportunity. She just needed some damn rest, but it would be hard knowing her little sister was out there, alone now.

MJ tucked the gun into his belt. The air around them still smelled like McDonald's.

"When do we deliver them? This feeding them crap is eating into our profits."

Luke, the sturdier man in this duo, twisted open the cap on a bottle of beer and used the cap to scratch at a spot on his beard.

"When we get ten, we have a full load. And they're paying five grand a pop, so that's fifty big ones. I think we can spare a few Big Macs."

"So we need four more?"

"That's what Marco said. Groups of ten."

Luke let himself fall onto the couch with an exhale and a grunt. Mid-thirties and already exhausted by the world. MJ still had four years to go until the big three-oh and acted every bit of the over-excited puppy he still was. Skinny from the excess energy he always burned in a thousand tiny ways. No amount of weight lifting ever added any bulk to his frame.

"I don't know why we need to go through him. We should just deliver them ourselves."

"The government only pays out if you have a contract. I applied, but I'm still waiting."

MJ sat down on the couch next to Luke, then jerked back up with a small yelp of pain. He reached around and took the gun out of his belt, set it on the side table, and sat back down.

"Fuckin' bureaucracy."

"It's all the goddamn libtards trying to block all the executive orders," Luke said, scratching at his whiskers with his fingers this time. "That shit is fair and legal and gives us permission to do the work those pussies haven't been able to do."

"Yeah, like take our country back."

"Fuckin' A." Luke raised his bottle of beer and toasted the air, then took a deep swig.

"I don't understand why they have to try to block everything the President does. All he's trying to do is make America great again."

"And he will. As soon as we get this scum off the streets. More jobs, no more stealing our taxes and services."

"The five grand a head ain't too bad, either."

Luke raised his bottle again. "Damn straight." The promise of the money had been so good, Luke quit his job working for a roofer. He planned to make bounty hunting for ICE a full-time gig. Then maybe shift into a real ICE gig down the road, get some of that health insurance and pension. The wait list for an official job had grown longer. Damn near every Proud Boy and Patriot Front soldier had signed on to get paid for what they fantasized about for years.

MJ shook his leg and picked at his fingernails, unable to sit still. Luke figured the kid had some form of ADHD or something. He usually jackhammered his knee up and down unconsciously, keeping the beat to some unheard rhythm in his head. Luke assumed it was very noisy in there.

He preferred keeping quiet, staying to himself. DON'T TREAD ON ME was not only tattooed across his back, but it was how he tried to live his life. He didn't like having these people on his property and wanted them gone as soon as he could. But for five thousand dollars apiece, they could stay for now. Finally, a good use of his tax dollars.

"So, four more?" MJ said. "When are we gonna go?"

"We can try tonight. I need a break, though. Just chill out for a bit."

"Yeah, yeah, no worries. I should go check in at home. My mom's probably worried. You know how she gets."

"Yeah, go see her. I'll meet you back at eight."

"Yeah, yeah, cool. Catch you later."

Luke didn't get up when MJ left. He settled back deeper into the couch cushions and drained the rest of his beer, then thought about opening another.

15

Highway 90 ran straight and flat as the truck moved due West. Ivana had checked her maps app and it said the trip would take them thirty hours with no stops. Carter took the first shift behind the wheel and he kept the truck at a steady seventy-five miles and hour.

They hadn't spoken in an hour, both lost in their thoughts. Carter wondering if this was the last time he'd see Minnesota, Ivana anticipating seeing her daughter again for the first time since she left home to start her new life in California, away from her father, who currently sat in a grave back in Bellington. A grave she'd never visited.

The days were still short, and the sun had dropped in front of them low on the horizon, but a long line of clouds kept the worst of it out of Carter's eyes. Ivana had checked a weather app, too, and there were no imminent snowstorms or anything that looked likely to delay them.

Chester curled between them on the bench seat, his jowls slack like uncooked dough spread out over the seat.

It kept happening that Carter found himself driving into something he wasn't sure he was prepared for. He didn't know what to expect, nor how he could help. But Bree had asked for his help, and he would always answer that call.

Driving into the unknown had become his mode of transportation in recent months.

The truck didn't ride what anyone would call smooth at that sustained speed. Carter clicked on the radio to hear something besides the incessant rattle of the bodywork. He spun the dial and stopped on song after song that he didn't recognize. Music had been the first thing to leave him behind in his age. It had abandoned him decades ago, and now it mocked him outwardly.

"You can pick what you like," he said.

Ivana spun the dial a few times and landed on a smooth R&B song that sounded vaguely familiar to Carter, but could have been that it sounded like a dozen other songs. She kept the volume low, like the singer was whispering a performance just for them.

"This is crazy, no?" she said.

"Crazy is where I live these days."

"I hope this girl is all right."

"I hope Katie and Bree are all right."

Ivana's eyes moved over the shadows growing longer on the cut fields bracketing the highway like acre-wide sheets of corduroy laid out over the land.

"They know how to stay out of trouble."

Carter wasn't so sure. He had been witness to a time when they were both in plenty of trouble.

"You ever been to California?"

"No. You?"

"Once. Took a trip to Los Angeles and San Diego with Ava. Before Audrey was born, so, ooh, a long time ago."

"Nice?"

"As I remember. Ava got a bad sunburn. Wasn't used to that much sunshine, I guess."

The song switched to a male voice crooning insincerely about love. Carter checked the dashboard.

"We've got enough gas to get us over into South Dakota, I think. We can stop there to fuel up, take a rest stop, and maybe switch. You should get some rest now."

"Okay. I'll try."

Carter patted Chester on his chest with a deep thumping sound.

"If you need any inspiration…"

She smiled, then leaned against the window and shut her eyes.

This time, the knock on the door was much more gentle. Bree opened it without any fear. She'd expected Mrs. Borgeson, the older lady who sometimes watched Marta. Word had gotten out about what happened to Isla, and she would want to check in on the child. Instead, she found Orlando, their coworker from Surfside Tacos, where both Bree and Katie had gotten jobs within two days of deciding to stay.

"Hey, Bree." Orlando was tall and skinny, limber in a way that reminded Bree of how palm trees bend in the wind. He had been trying to grow a mustache for months now and had only managed a light dusting of whiskers. He turned twenty in a month, and when he did, he promised himself that he would finally ask Katie out on a date. Until then, he acted like a lovelorn puppy whenever he was around her. His crush was a secret to no one.

He held two bags of food.

"I brought Katie some soup. And stuff for you, too."

"Soup?"

"She called out sick, so I figured this would make her feel better."

Bree opened the door wide for Orlando to come inside. "She called out, but she's not sick."

Katie came out from the bedroom where she'd been reading to Marta. "Hey."

"You're not sick?" Orlando asked.

"No. Why?"

"Oh." He looked embarrassed. Bree had to step in and rescue him.

"He brought us food."

She took the bags and brought them to the kitchen counter.

Orlando acted as the unofficial assistant manager, since the real manager was his cousin, even though Julio was never around. Bree couldn't remember the last time she saw him inside the restaurant. The two chefs were second or maybe third cousins. Neither one knew that much about cooking, but it didn't seem to matter. Surfside Tacos had a loyal local following. Even if they weren't going to go wide with franchises anytime soon, they did a fine business.

Bree explained the bullet points of Marta staying with them and Isla being taken, the real reason Katie had called out for her shift.

"Damn, man," he said. "Those goddamn ICE guys are everywhere. Like cockroaches."

"More like that's what they think of us," Katie said.

Bree couldn't say much. She was the most fair-skinned girl in town and the last on any ICE target list for deportation.

"Well, that's super nice of you guys to take her in like that. For how long, do you think?"

"We don't know," Katie said. "Their parents can be gone for months at a time. But we have a sort of a plan."

Bree gave her a look like she'd spilled a secret.

"What?" Katie said. "It's fine. It's just Orlando."

He looked like he'd been stabbed by a knife. He wanted to be anyone but *just* Orlando to her.

Katie explained that a friend from back in Minnesota was coming to help. She left out any of the more violent details of what happened and how they came to know Carter, but assured Orlando that he would be the one to resolve this.

"Okay, cool. You know you can always call me when things go wrong, too. I can be useful."

"I know that," she said, placating him with sympathetic eyes lacking any hint of a come-on. "But he's done, like, this sort of thing before. Kinda."

"All right," he said. "Let's eat."

The truck stop rose up from the flat South Dakota plains, a neon-lit oasis, bright and busy as an airport. Signs flashed a lurid sales pitch to passing truckers and weary travelers. Essentials—gas, food, bathrooms—drew people off the highway like animals gathered around a watering hole. Truck engines rumbled and mixed with treble-heavy speakers playing country music and the steady wash of vehicles passing on the highway, somehow not tempted to stop despite the desperate electrical seduction that cast a glow against the low clouds overhead.

Carter's pickup sounded like an asthmatic after a five-mile run.

He bypassed the gas pumps and found a parking space outside the cluster of restaurants offering food co-opted from other countries and deep-fried into American cuisine.

He turned the truck off, and it gave a final death rattle exhale that sounded like a downed grizzly bear breathing its last.

"We'll let her rest a little while. I guess we should eat."

Ivana peered out the window at her options. "I packed some."

"Something tells me it's better than any of this."

Ivana smiled weakly at the thin compliment.

Carter got Chester down and walked him to the edge of the asphalt for a bathroom break. He could use one himself, but the dog took priority. He could live in discomfort easily after all the practice he'd gotten the past few months. It was daylight bright, and the constant noise made it feel like a factory floor. Trucks came and went, some idled on the far edge of the lot where drivers had stopped to bed down for the night. Carter spotted a girl with short bleached-blonde hair, a shorter denim skirt, and a puffy fake-fur jacket on top. He knew what her business was without asking. A truck stop along Interstate 90 in South Dakota had to be as far from streetwalking in Manhattan or Los Angeles as you could get, but just like the chain restaurants, there was always an appetite for what she was selling.

Carter tried to stretch his back muscles. He twisted and leaned and managed to work out some of the kinks. When Chester finished, they walked back to the truck. Ivana had laid out a meal for them on the dashboard. Carter went to start the truck to have the heater on, but the engine gave nothing but tired groans.

"Well, shit."

He turned the key forward, then back, then forward again. Each time the truck gave it her all, but could not catch a spark. The sustained highway drive had done her in.

"What do we do now?" Ivana asked.

"There's gotta be someone around here who can fix it."

"At this hour?"

"I'll see."

He ate quickly and left Ivana to feed Chester. "Not too much cheese." She nodded, but he knew the old dog would get whatever he wanted off of Ivana, the soft touch.

Carter walked toward the shop, which sold motor oil, windshield wipers, air fresheners, and all manner of car accessories. He saw the working girl walking with a trucker toward the line of idling big rigs. At least she'd have the benefit of a heater inside a truck cab.

* * *

Ivana hand-fed Chester. He took whatever she offered from her hand and barely chewed. Her hand became slick with slobber, but she didn't mind.

"You're a good boy. I'm glad we didn't leave you behind."

She gave him another morsel. He swallowed that and waited patiently for the next.

"How's he doing, huh? He doesn't tell me. He's stubborn, but you know that."

Chester licked his jowls.

"It seems silly, but I wasn't even thinking of it until the truck, you know? All I can think of is Katie. But this old truck…that old man. Nothing can run forever, huh?"

She scratched his ears. He grumbled a bit, not wanting the dinner to end.

"I think he's okay. I tell myself he's okay. We need him, right?"

She kissed Chester on the top of his head.

* * *

Carter made an overdue visit to the men's room. His stomach cramped and his body ached, but most of that could have been from the long drive. Still many more hours to go, but being a passenger would be easier on him. He could use the sleep, too. Sleeping usually made the worst attacks of his own body in revolt fade away.

He walked the aisles of the auto supply store, found a worker to ask about getting his truck looked at. The guy looked at his watch. As bright as it was inside, Carter figured he genuinely had no idea the time.

"Nah, not this late. Morning though. Eight a.m."

"We're kind of in a hurry. Gotta make the West Coast."

"Sorry, man. Nothing I can do unless you want a set of truck nuts or Waylon Jennings greatest hits on cassette. I got No-Doz and condoms, too. This time of night, those are our best sellers."

"Thanks anyway."

Carter bought three large bottles of water and thought seriously about the Waylon Jennings tape. Back outside, the girl in the denim skirt walked back across the lot already. She moved fast on her high heels, the faux fur coat in one hand. The trucker followed close behind, shouting insults at her.

"You don't like it, you can always jerk off, pal," she said, not turning around.

A lover's quarrel, even when money was involved. *Men and women, oil and water*, Carter mused. How had he gotten so lucky with Ava?

She angled toward the bank of restrooms and showers. A sign laid out the policy for truckers—time limits, rules about what areas you could go without clothes on. Carter figured there had to be complaints before that rule was implemented.

The trucker moved as quick as he could, but Carter noticed he wasn't wearing shoes. He was bulky, too. Thick and solid, like he might crush her if their coupling had been consummated. Clearly, she bailed before anything had happened.

"Get back here, you bitch. I ain't paying for nothing."

"You wasted my time. Now fuck off."

She vanished into the hallway leading to the restrooms. He followed. Carter walked back to the truck.

Inside, he set the waters down, and Ivana asked, "What was that all about?"

"A breach of contract of some sort," he said. "I didn't get the details."

He kept an eye on the entrance to the bathrooms. He didn't like the red-faced look on the trucker. The girl appeared very slight with him chasing her down, a grizzly bear in pursuit of a gazelle.

In an act of optimism, he tried the key again. The engine turned over, the old gal giving it one last try.

"Oh, thank God," Ivana said.

Carter grinned at her, but didn't let on how little confidence he had in the truck making it all the way to California. He let the engine idle while the heater warmed up. They needed gas, but he didn't want to shut the engine off again. Maybe if she warmed up and he promised to take it easy, the old gal would cooperate.

The trucker came out of the bathroom hallway, making a straight line for his truck. He marched angrily, a scowl still on his face, and he muttered to himself. Carter looked back to the doorway, but the girl didn't emerge.

He took a sip of water, then capped the bottle.

"I'll be right back."

Carter watched the trucker retreat across the lot, his heavy-footed plodding moving slow but steady like a tank rolling over uneven ground. He paused at the open entry to the hallway and peered inside. He saw nothing;

a sound like a wounded bird reverberated off the tile floors and walls. He ventured in.

"Hello?"

He followed the sound until he reached the Women's room. The door stood open, and he could hear crying.

"Is everything okay?"

When she didn't answer, Carter leaned in. The girl sat with her back to a tile wall, the fur coat torn and cast off to the side like roadkill. The contents of her purse were spilled over the tile floor, and a thin trickle of blood came from her nose.

Carter bent down to her.

"Sorry, man. Closed for business tonight."

"I'm just here to see if you're okay."

"I guess."

She put a hand in his, and he helped her to her feet. She exhaled deeply, resigned to the assault. The price of doing business.

The girl checked her face in the mirror and scowled at the blood.

"May I help you?"

"If you want. I can't pay you; he took it all. And no *favors* for payment either, get me?"

"Those days are behind me."

She coughed out a small laugh. "Ever since the little blue pill, you'd be surprised."

Carter gathered items from the floor and dumped them back into her bag. When he handed it to her, she said, "You really are just being nice, aren't you?"

"Is that so strange?"

"Buddy, you have no idea."

He held out a hand. "Carter McCoy."

She shook it. "Dazzle." She made a sour face and reconsidered. "Diana, actually. The other is just for business."

"You gonna be okay?"

She let out a long sigh. "He's gonna talk shit all over this place. Kill all my business. All over me not wanting to…" She stopped herself. "Let's just say a slight dispute in the kind of services I render, and those I do not."

"Enough said."

"Either way, this place is dead for me now. Time to move on, which won't be the worst thing."

"Can we drop you someplace? We're headed west."

"Who's we?"

"My friend and I. And my dog."

Diana eyeballed him with a lifetime of distrust.

"Nothing weird," he reassured her. "Just offering a ride. If not, I'll be on my way."

"Okay. I'll ride with you. Y'know, you remind me of my granddad."

"I think I do that for a lot of people."

They walked out together, leaving her torn coat behind.

In the truck, introductions were made, and Ivana squeezed down to make room for Diana, though the fit was tight. Chester ended up on Ivana's lap with his head leaning on Diana, who cooed and baby-talked him while she scratched his ears.

"Oh my god, you're just the cutest ever."

"That's Chester," Carter said.

"Oh, yes, you handsome boy."

Carter looked across at the truck still idling on the far end of the lot. The driver was inside, warm and likely guilt-free. For more than 70 years of his life, Carter would drive away and never think of the man again. But things had changed in the last several months. And if men like him never suffered any consequence, things would never change for them.

"I'll be right back," he said.

Carter went into the auto supply store, found a red five-gallon gas can. He walked to the pumps and filled it.

Ivana and Diana watched as he walked off-balance across the lot toward the truck, the gas can pulling him down on the right side of his body.

"What's he doing?" Diana asked.

"I think I know," Ivana said. "There's something you should know about

Carter."

* * *

The truck sat by itself, at least three empty spaces between the next big rig. The corner of the lot was dim compared to the rest of the sprawling truck stop. A decent place to get some rest, and an even better one to take out your kinks and knock around a woman.

Also a good place for a fire.

Carter uncapped the gas can and began to pour. He made circles around the tires, splashed the door, the headlights, the front bumper. He left a long line leading away from the truck until the can was empty, then tossed it aside. He removed the lighter he'd bought inside. Stepping carefully to avoid the pools of gasoline, he walked to the cab of the truck. He pounded three times on the driver's door, then backed away.

Carter flicked the lighter and got it going, bent down, and touched the gas. Flames took off running while he walked the other direction.

* * *

Ivana slid into the driver's seat. "Yeah, that's what I thought."

Diana sat slack-jawed as flames sprouted all around the semi. There was no explosion, no twenty-foot flames reaching the sky. It was a pleasant winter campfire, but with an acrid chemical smell, very far from fresh pine logs.

Carter hurried in something short of a run and reached his pickup as the driver came tumbling out of his truck. Carter squeezed in beside Diana, and they all took a moment to follow the action like it was a TV show. The trucker ran in circles, shouting curses at the flames, swatting at them with a shirt like a surrender flag in his hand.

Ivana put the truck in gear and backed out. She switched to drive and aimed for the exit back into the highway, hoping for another option for gas not too far down the road. The pickup coughed, shuddered, and died.

"Shit," Carter said.

"What?" Diana asked.

"Truck's dead."

"Shit," she said.

Other truckers had come out of their cabs to help fight the flames. Two had small extinguishers they blasted at the tires and the front grille, all while the sturdy man ran around shouting the same insults he had at Diana.

"What do we do?" Ivana asked.

"Hang on." Diana pushed past Carter and climbed over him to get out. She ran in bare feet across the asphalt. Nobody had seen Carter with his gas can, and nobody looked their way now, all attention on the burning truck. Chester sat up and regarded the commotion with a curious tilt to his head.

Two minutes later, the blast of an air horn sounded. A semi truck pulled alongside the pickup, and Diana leaned out from the passenger window.

"Get in," she said.

Carter helped Chester down, Ivana grabbed their luggage. They were up and inside the spacious cab of a Peterbilt, and the portly driver with a receding hairline and a mischievous glint in his eye said, "I'm Larry. Let's get out of dodge."

Carter turned to watch his pickup truck fade away as they pulled out of the lot and made toward the highway. A tugging loss pulled at his insides, and worried he was having one of his attacks, but it was only the pain of losing a friend. The truck had been his for more than three decades, carried he and Ava out to dinner and the movies, hauled heavy things in her rusty and dented bed, been a witness to Carter's life longer than nearly anyone or anything in his life. Now he left her behind, alone and lifeless in a Vegas-bright parking lot on the side of the highway. He knew it would be a miracle if he ever sat on her lumpy spring seats again.

He never thought he'd outlive the truck, or much else in this world. But they were moving again, headed west, still alive.

Luke fantasized about the first thing he would spend his money on. He couldn't pick between a new TV, a new pistol, or a custom paint job for the van. He ruled the van out first. If he had anything too flashy, it would be too easy to notice. With the plain white wrap on the van as it stood, they could roll into any neighborhood, any parking lot, any business, and be anonymous. It helped when they took the illegals into custody.

Tonight had been a bust, though. Not one capture. The President's policies were working, at least. Fewer illegal immigrants on the streets. Less of a scourge on the community. He had read where crime stats hadn't dropped the way they expected, but it was a matter of time. Those data points played out over months. And all the newspapers liked to report on were things like that youth pastor who got arrested for having photos from a hidden camera in the showers at the Christian day camp he ran. The media ignored all the immigrants murdering, kidnapping, selling fentanyl. They were probably complicit, getting a kickback from the cartels for ignoring the story.

Luke nodded along, agreeing with the argument going on in his head, his theories based on nothing except what he wished were true.

"I'm hungry," MJ said.

"Yeah, I could eat."

It was past ten p.m., late for this sleepy beach town. The only places open this late were a few lonely taco stands on the East side of town.

"Tacos?" Luke asked.

MJ hesitated like he knew he should say no, but he gave in. They both loved tacos. When Mama Rosa's had closed down because Rosa herself got deported, Luke had been bummed, though he never said it out loud.

"You ever feel like, we're kinda like exterminators?" MJ asked.

"How do you mean?"

"We, like, do the same thing. Getting rid of the insects. Like, if you had bugs crawling all over your house, or rats or something, you'd call an exterminator. Well, we're like that, but we've been called by the White House, and he hired us to get things back to right."

"Yeah, I guess so."

MJ put a foot on the dashboard, smiling smugly with his new theory.

"Hey, what about her?"

Luke followed where MJ pointed. A woman with short, cropped hair and dark brown skin walked with her hands stuffed in the pockets of her coat. She moved with purpose and gave off an air of *don't mess with me.*

"Wasn't born here, that's for damn sure," MJ said.

Luke checked his mirrors quick and made a U-turn. He pulled the van a few feet ahead of where she was walking and put it in park, leaving the engine on. They both pulled black gaiters up from their necks to cover their mouths and noses, leaving only their eyes visible. MJ got out and blocked her path on the sidewalk. Luke came around.

"You got ID?" Luke asked.

Up close, the woman wasn't Mexican. Indian, he guessed. Or some other country from over there. When she spoke, she confirmed it with her slight South Asian accent.

"You talking to me?"

"Yeah, you. Speak English?"

"I just spoke English, dipshit."

MJ eased slowly to the side and then moved to stand behind her, boxing her in between them.

"We're immigration enforcement. You're gonna have to come with us."

"Uh, I don't think so."

MJ spoke up from behind her, and she turned her body so she could see both of them. "Hey, no more attitude. We got orders from the President."

"What orders? You got a warrant? You got badges?"

Luke dug in his pants pocket and pulled out the polished steel badge he'd gotten off eBay. It looked official and was, at one time, in another state for another job. He flashed it quickly, moving it in his hand so she couldn't read the words embossed on the shield. HARLAN COUNTY FIRE INSPECTOR.

"Don't make this difficult."

"I'm a fucking U.S. citizen, you asshole," she said. "Go harass someone else."

Luke and MJ locked eyes and wordlessly asked each other what to do next. If she was a citizen, then she wouldn't be deported. All that would be sorted out at the processing center. And that would all happen after Luke collected the bounty. They paid the five grand per head upon receipt, not upon deportation. If she was telling the truth, she'd be out in a couple of weeks. An inconvenience, sure, but worth it for the five grand she'd bring in. And who knows, maybe she had a record. Maybe she was lying. They'd figure all that out down at the processing center near the border.

Luke stepped forward and put a hand on her elbow. "Come with us, ma'am."

She jerked away. "Get your fucking hands off me."

Turned to face Luke, MJ could reach into his jacket and take out the zip ties without her noticing. He could step up behind her without her moving away, and he could slip the loop over one wrist and then twist her free arm behind her before she could do anything about it. With a practiced motion, MJ had the woman in cuffs.

"Hey!"

Luke slid open the side door to the van, and MJ pushed the woman toward the opening. She spewed a steady stream of profanity and insults to them, their mothers, their political party.

Once inside, she tumbled to the floor, and Luke slammed home the door, trapping her inside. They were getting better at this part of it. Faster, smoother from initial contact to apprehension. In the event she was telling the truth, then he felt a little bad. But five grand could help smooth over an awful lot of bad feelings.

The truck was basically a one-bedroom apartment on wheels. Behind the front seats was a bench seat in back and then a sleeping cubby complete with a full-size mattress and curtains. Chester claimed that right away, and Carter apologized.

"It's all right," Larry said. "Let the ol boy get comfortable."

Diana had gone on in an excited ramble about how Carter had taken the gas can and torched the truck of the man who'd assaulted her. Larry listened in wide-eyed astonishment.

"Can't say he didn't deserve it," he said.

"Glad you think so," Carter said. "I didn't know if there was some code of honor among drivers."

"Not when they're assholes. And not when they do anything like that to Dazzle here."

If Larry used her professional name, Carter assumed he knew how they came to be acquainted.

"She's like a daughter to me," Larry said.

Maybe Carter was wrong.

"I always check in on her when I swing through."

"Knowing Larry is like having a chaperone to the dance," Diana said.

"Well," Carter said. "I guess we're lucky you were passing through."

An hour had gone by, and both Ivana and Diana had fallen asleep on the bench seat behind them. Chester snored in the comfort of the bed, being rocked slowly by the rhythm of the highway at seventy-five miles an hour.

Larry had a calm ease to him that Carter admired, like a mall Santa on his off season. His resting face had a slight grin to it, always. He never got angry at passing motorists who cut him off, or left high beams on. He was easy to be around, charming and comforting as an old sweater. He seemed to know it, too.

"I hope we're not messing with your schedule," Carter said.

"Nah." Larry waved him off. "I like driving at night. I got vampire hours. Drive all night, sleep in the day. Less traffic that way. Just used to it, I guess."

The quiet buzz of 70s and 80s hard rock turned down low on the stereo covered the drone of eighteen wheels on the pavement. ZZ Top were touting the beauty of a woman's legs and her ability to use them.

"So, you make a habit of lighting trucks on fire?"

Carter said no, but he failed to elaborate. Picking up riders was dangerous enough without learning the one sitting next to you had killed a half dozen men in the past few months.

"I'm old enough I got no patience for assholes anymore."

"These days, you got plenty to choose from."

"That's why I have to make it to California. An old friend is in need."

"And they called you, the human torch?"

Carter smiled. "Different kind of help, but another woman in need."

"Then I'm happy to get you there. Folks gotta help each other, I say. Not enough of that going around these days."

The highway ran flat and straight, the cars and other trucks few and far between. Carter understood what Larry liked about driving at night.

"Kinda feels like driving through space, don't it?" Larry pointed out ahead of them to where it faded into nothing but black. No buildings or lights on either side of the road, no discernible horizon. Carter had to admit, it did look like empty space.

"Wish I could do that light speed jump, like in *Star Wars*. I like the life, but if I could get where I'm going in seconds flat, I'd take it."

"Yeah, I don't know."

"You wouldn't want light speed? No more waiting for things?"

Carter scratched at his chin. "I guess I'm not so anxious for things to speed up anymore. I'll get where I'm going fast enough, I suppose."

"Fair enough."

The song switched, and Foreigner warned them that things were urgent. They sailed on into the featureless void ahead of them.

33

Isla jolted awake as the door slid open. The heavy steel-reinforced door rolled on tracks bolted to the ceiling. Some industrial behemoth built to keep things out, repurposed to keep things in.

The older couple still huddled together in the corner, and the three younger ones sat up as one. MJ stood with his gun ready, but pointed down at the concrete floor. Luke pushed the new woman forward. She stumbled, hard to catch herself with her hands zip-tied behind her back. Isla and the others still wore their zip ties, but in front.

Without a word, the door slammed shut again, and they all listened to the chorus of locks and deadbolts being thrown.

Isla stood and went to the new woman.

"Are you okay?"

She was Indian, not Mexican. Isla wasn't sure if their two captors could even tell the difference.

"I'm okay, I guess. Not happy about this bullshit." She looked around the converted garage at the frightened faces looking back at her, the sparse square room with hard floors, bare walls, a sink, and little else. "What the fuck is this place?"

"They say they work for ICE," Isla said.

"This is no ICE facility."

"They're getting ready to take us to one," she said. "I heard them say something about getting ten people. My name is Isla."

"Deepti." She made a habitual motion to shake hands, but stopped when her arms would not comply.

They went around the room and made introductions. The older couple were Juan and Carlotta. The three others were Leo, Julia, and Nic.

"How long have you been here?" Deepti asked.

"Two days now," Isla said.

"It's fucking kidnapping."

"They keep talking about authority and executive orders. Not much we can do."

"Oh, I'll find something."

The others settled back into their positions, keeping mostly quiet except for some mumbled conversations in Spanish between them.

Isla stayed standing with Deepti, trying to welcome her.

"Someone will notice you're gone. They'll call the authorities."

"They *are* the authorities," Deepti said. "At least they're playing at it. Shit, I read about this happening, but I wasn't sure it was real. Not here anyway. Maybe in, like, Alabama or some place."

"My sister is the one I'm worried about. She's only twelve. I don't know what she'll do without me."

"I don't have kids, not married. Work will notice I don't show up, but they won't call anyone for a few days, and by then…"

"Feels helpless."

Deepti shook her head. "That's what they want. They act tough, they muscle us around. But fuck that. They picked up the wrong bitch."

Isla stood back as Deepti stalked the room, looking in all the corners, searching for a weakness. For the first time, she let herself think there might be a way out.

Luke got on the phone.

"Who're you calling?" MJ asked.

"Marco."

Marco had been the one to first suggest to Luke that he get in on the lucrative business of rounding up illegals. Ex-military, Marco gave the impression he was one step away from declaring a sovereign state. If he'd been more organized, he'd have run a militia, but instead he liked to complain a lot and do little about it. After the executive orders had been signed, Marco was first in line to start bounty hunting. He used a former Marine contact of his to create his own pipeline to ICE and start collecting suspected illegals off the streets.

"Hey, what's up?" Marco said.

"Hey, man. Look, I almost got a full load but, man, I gotta ask you…"

"Ask me what?"

Luke turned away from MJ so he could speak in private.

"Two of them keep saying they're citizens. Born here. Like, what do I do with that?"

"Are they?"

"How the hell should I know? You told me to pick up anyone within reasonable doubt of being illegal." Use your judgment, he'd been told. But grab them if they're brown.

Marco filled the line with a long sigh. "Luke, man, you gotta be smart about it. But hey, whatever their status, they'll sort it out at ICE. If they got the right papers, then no harm, no foul. They get released."

"But is that, like, legal?"

Another sigh. "If it happens under the executive order, then anything is legal. Shit, dude, if the J-sixers all got let go, what the hell are they gonna do to patriots like us? Nothing, man. Plus, did you see what the Supremes said about it? We're golden, man."

"So, I shouldn't worry that they've seen our faces and stuff?"

"I told you to keep that shit covered."

"We do when we're on patrol, but at the house…"

"You'll be fine. Once ICE gets them, it's not your problem anymore."

"Okay, that's what I thought. Just had to check."

"So when will you have a full load?"

"Tomorrow, probably."

"Okay. You let me know, and I'll add them to my next run."

"Hey, Marco, you think I can come along? I'd love to meet this guy, get some face time."

"No way, man. He's a busy guy. They got a full house. Miller's got his quotas, y'know? You let me deal with him. Just keep feeding me the goods, and I'll deliver them and get you paid."

Shut down again. Marco protected his contacts at ICE, but always collected his percentage of Luke's take. It was easy to see that Luke had no chance of cutting Marco out and going direct to the big man. Money was on the line, and that Luke could understand and almost forgive. Any time either fear or questions about the legality of what he was doing crept in, the money always brought Luke back.

"Yeah, all right. Call you soon."

The sun rose at their backs, painting the rocky mountains in orange and red. The sky over the West coast ahead of them stayed a blue-black like being twenty feet underwater.

Carter stirred from his sleep when the truck downshifted, and the steady rocking of highway speed slowed. Larry yawned for the first time all trip, like the rising sun had set off an alarm and his body knew it was time for sleep.

"Get a few winks?" Larry asked.

"A few." Carter turned and saw that the women were still sleeping, and Chester had barely moved all night. Four adults in the truck, and not one had bothered to move the dog from the only real bed.

"It's my time to shut down for a few hours," Larry said.

He eased the truck into a parking space along a long row of other trucks. They'd made it to Wyoming overnight. The landscape had gone from flat and filled with dark stones to dramatic peaks and wide grasslands. But the truck stops all looked the same.

The women woke up, and plans were made to reconvene in a few hours.

"I don't need much," Larry said. "Four or five hours ought to do it."

"I'm gonna split," Diana said. "Set up shop here for a while."

"Okay. I'll look in on you on my way back through," Larry said.

Carter rousted Chester and lifted him down from the truck. "Sorry if he farted on your bedsheets."

Larry laughed. "Hell, what do you think I'm gonna do with them?"

Out on the tarmac, Carter took Chester for a bathroom break and urged the dog to hurry up so he could do the same.

Ivana hugged Diana. "Thank you so much."

"No, thank *you* guys. That was so badass, what he did."

"We would have been screwed if we didn't get a ride."

"Yeah, Larry's great. Good luck with your trip. You go get that girl, bring her home."

Ivana had told her the basics. Diana had looked off with a melancholy stare out into the black night, and Ivana knew right then that Diana understood a thing or two about a girl going missing and someone taking advantage of her. She didn't press.

Carter came back, handed the leash vote to Ivana, and also hugged Diana.

"Thanks, Carter."

"My pleasure. Nice to meet you."

"Some days, y'know, it's easy to think all men are creeps. But now and then…"

"Happy to be one who sets your mind at ease."

"Never at ease. But a little less cynical."

Diana walked away with her one bag over her shoulder.

Carter turned to Ivana. "Gotta pee, then coffee. Then let's call the girls."

"Sounds good."

* * *

Visiting the toilet hadn't been a fun experience for a while. A dull pain came with it each time, and lately it had been growing in intensity, like the red line of a thermometer climbing higher through August.

It took a while of Carter standing there to get things going, and when they did, he winced. Traces of red filled the bowl. Carter flushed it away quickly and tried to put it out of his mind.

Bree dropped Marta off at school. She didn't like the way the moms in their minivans and SUVs gave her a side-eyed look as if she were a teen mom with a twelve-year-old. She wanted to scream out the window that she would have had to have been nine years old when she had Marta to be her mom, and they can mind their own fucking business.

Her shift at Surfside Tacos didn't start until three, but she had a plan for what to do with her morning.

Orlando had told stories about the fear running through the community since the start of the ICE abductions. They'd targeted a few places multiple times. Places where people gathered looking for day work. Anything from house cleaning to painting to junk removal. Anything they could hire out for the day and make enough to get by until the next day. Some people talk about living paycheck to paycheck, where these people lived sunrise to sunrise. Why anyone, let alone a government, would target hard-working people who were struggling, Bree didn't understand.

She drove to a dusty parking lot in front of a sun-bleached mini-mall with a laundromat, a check cashing place, a Chinese restaurant, and a hardware store that looked sandblasted and nearly vacant.

She parked and got out. Three men in jeans and pearl-button shirts stood in a cluster at the far end of the lot. Weeds sprouted from cracks in the pavement like a teenage boy trying to grow a beard. A muffled speaker played *Tejano* music through the open door of the laundromat even though nobody was inside.

The men noticed her and one pointed her way. She ignored them and kept her focus on the road. At ten to eight in the morning, traffic was light, the businesses other than the laundromat still closed and the air cool. She didn't know what she hoped to find—a line of transport trucks and men in camouflage herding lines of migrants in handcuffs? From the news reports she'd seen, some raids were twenty men in six or seven vehicles, a shock and awe show of force. Nobody showed badges, and everyone hid their faces.

Others, like the one that had swept up Isla, were solo vehicles and only a few men. Renegades, mercenaries. The ones you really had to be afraid of, since they didn't always follow the rules, and the whole idea of rules was a concept quickly fading into the past. People had been killed, and the idea of consequences for it was far off and foreign.

It was hard to imagine what it would be like to live in fear of simply walking the streets, but the fear was the point.

As she tried to think what she'd do if she did see people being taken, and how she had no actual plan if that happened, she noticed the three men getting closer to her.

Her defenses went up. She told herself it wasn't that they were Mexican, or some other south-of-the-border heritage. She wanted to end the persecution of these people, so she couldn't be afraid of them, right? Right?

They walked toward her in a direct line, not hiding that they were coming. Bree exhaled and reminded herself that they didn't automatically mean her any harm, and if she assumed that, she was as bad as *them*.

"Hey, chica."

They formed a V, and the man at the point spoke. He wore a tightly trimmed goatee, hair slicked back. His tanned skin had already started to wrinkle from the sun, even though she pegged him for being in his twenties. All three men wore cowboy boots and were ready for any hard labor that came their way.

"You sightseeing?" he said. "Checking out the exotic locals?"

"What? I'm just...don't worry about it."

"I know a white girl like you isn't looking for work."

The two men behind him smiled and let out a dusty chuckle.

"Maybe she's looking to hire someone," the young man to his right said.

"She needs someone to treat her right."

The three closed in on her. Bree backed up until she pressed against the glass of the laundromat. She glanced over her shoulder to confirm there was nobody inside. Empty. She was alone in the parking lot with these men. No cameras from the local businesses. Too cheap for that. It's what made it a perfect place to grab people off the streets.

A small pang of guilt echoed through Bree because she knew coming here held no fear for herself, a pale Midwestern white girl, of being abducted. Her lack of fear had led her into danger.

"Is that right?" the goateed man said. "You looking for a little of that good-good? That sweet D?"

Bree exhaled, and a calm came over her. These weren't organized predators. These weren't the gang bangers Washington wanted her to believe roamed the streets hunting for women like her. These were horny 20-somethings like she'd seen a hundred times before. Typical assholes with too much pent-up testosterone and time on their hands. They were nothing to be feared.

Bree let her hand drift to her back pocket.

"I'm not looking for anything, guys."

"Maybe not looking, but you found it. Come on, Chica, take a walk on the wild side. You ever had three at once before?"

Bree's hand came out quickly, thumbing open the knife blade as it went.

Ever since the trouble back home, she'd taken to carrying a knife. Even before the violence of that summer, she distrusted most men her age, she took a cynical view of the world and expected tragedy to befall her. But when she and Carter set things in motion, and it worked, she realized she needed to be her own savior when it counted and vowed never to be a victim again.

From the look in Goatee's eyes, he wasn't seeing a victim in front of him.

"Back off," she said. "You get one warning."

The tip of the knife barely trembled, which Bree couldn't believe because inside, she was freaking out. All three men took a step back, and Goatee raised his hands in surrender.

"Relax, chica. You looked like you wanted some action, is all."

"I looked like I wanted to mind my own fucking business, which is what you should assume with every woman you see." Bree leaned forward, pushing the knife close to his face, the tip aimed at his eyeball. "And every woman you see for the rest of your life, you limp dick piece of shit."

"Man, fuck her," one of the others said, and he turned quickly and began walking away. The others followed. Goatee made a kissing sound and gave her a wink. He hadn't learned a thing. Maybe the next woman would stab him. If so, he deserved it.

Bree folded the knife and slid it back into her pocket. She gave one last look around the parking lot and realized how foolish it was for her to even have come here. There is no world in which she was going to stop armed government agents from doing whatever the hell they wanted. Her little knife might work on some playground bullies, but not on a real threat. She needed a plan, though. Being idle was horrible. Knowing Isla was out there and Marta was alone, it killed her. She needed to do something. She needed Carter to get there.

Isla had managed to get some sleep, but was up now with the sun. She only knew the time from the yellowed plastic wall clock tilted at an angle above the sink. They had taken their cell phones, any personal belongings, and IDs before anyone was put inside the holding cell.

She wanted a shower and a change of clothes desperately. The more things dragged on, the more Isla came to understand that the two men holding them were amateurs, not very good at it, and behind schedule.

Deepti had resisted falling asleep until very late. She finally succumbed and still had her eyes shut and mouth slack. The older couple, Juan and Carlotta, were awake as well. When they realized Isla had woken, they nodded and gave a slight smile, but still kept to themselves on the other side of the room, never letting go of each other. In a different scenario, it would have been sweet and romantic.

Everyone else jolted awake when the door slid open. Luke and MJ shoved in three more people—two women and a young man. They moved in stunned silence, resigned to their fate after seeing so many reports of deportations and what happened to people in ICE custody. Seeing others there in zip-tie handcuffs delivered a knockout blow to any hope they may have held on to.

Early mornings were the best hunting times. People gathered to wait for work, hoping to join a construction crew or find someone looking for a day laborer. They knew if they wanted a shot at being picked, they had to get there first. They got picked, all right.

"We roll out in a half hour," Luke said. "Get ready."

The door slammed shut.

Isla didn't know what kind of getting ready they could do. They had nothing to pack, no calls to make.

"What's that mean, roll out?" Deepti asked.

"It means we're going to the larger ICE detention center," Isla said. "I heard them talking about it."

"At least there they have to let us talk to a lawyer, right?"

Isla shrugged. The idea of legal due process wasn't a guarantee any longer.

Chatter in Spanish started among the new people and the younger three. Explanations were made, or attempted at least. Nobody knew a whole lot of details about what was happening to them, but they were eager to speculate and imagine several worst-case scenarios.

When Luke and MJ returned, they had a tall and broad man with them dressed in camouflage. He was deeply tanned with a short beard over a heavy jawline. Isla noticed MJ call him Marco.

"So what do you think?"

"Nice haul," Marco said. "Let's get 'em loaded up."

"God damn," MJ said. "Fifty grand."

"Forty," Marco said. "After my fee."

Isla noticed the gun in MJ's hand.

"Your fee?"

Luke held out a hand when he could feel MJ's heat rising. "We talked about this."

"Yeah, but ten grand just for transport?"

"Hey," Marco said. He stood square against MJ, stiff and straight like a military review. "I got the contacts, I made the arrangements, I facilitated the payment."

MJ quickly backed down. "Whatever, dude."

Deepti stepped forward, her arms still behind her back, cinched in zip-ties. "So, you're in charge around here? I knew it couldn't be these two dipshits."

Marco studied her. "You're not Mexican."

"Brilliant. Yes, there are a hundred and eight other countries in the world. Bravo. Now, when do I get a phone call to talk to a lawyer?"

Marco laughed. "When Uncle Sam says you can."

Deepti moved even closer. Isla flashed her eyes over to MJ's gun again. She worried that Deepti carried too much attitude with her as she closed the gap between her and the men in charge. She moved slowly with what Isla might describe as a swagger. If it was an act, it was a good one.

"The constitution says I get a lawyer. Last I checked, that was a big deal to your Uncle Sam. Y'know, the founding document?"

Marco loomed over her, set his feet shoulder-width apart, and folded his hands behind his back, mirroring her. "Executive Order 14159, issued by the President of these United States, says you can shut the fuck up and do what I tell you to do. And it says illegals can and will be deported faster than you can cook up some vindaloo. So get in the van, sister."

Luke stepped forward and put a hand on the arm of Carlotta, eager to get things moving.

"Okay, let's go. Faster they get out of here, the faster we get paid."

Carlotta hesitated and pulled against Luke. She gave a look over her shoulder to Juan, pleading and fear in her eyes. She gripped his hand, fingers interlaced in his. Luke pulled, and their hands slipped apart. Carlotta let out a sound of physical pain, as if a part of her own body had been ripped away. Juan said, *"Mi esposa,"* and reached after her, but Luke yanked her out of reach.

Isla could see Juan think for a second. She wanted to scream out to him to stay put, not to try anything. She stayed quiet.

Juan pushed off the wall and shoulder-checked Luke. The cowboy hat flipped off his head as he moved stiffly and awkwardly, like he was trying to remember the steps to a dance. He gave a sort of karate chop downward onto Luke's arm to release Carlotta. The six young people started chattering like hens in a coop.

Luke spun off of Carlotta and nearly tumbled to the ground. When he stood up straight, Juan came at him and bear hugged him, shouting in Spanish. Carlotta fell back, in tears now and shouting for Juan to stop. She reached out to him, only wanting his touch again to feel safe.

Isla moved to step forward, but Marco's bulk stood between her and the scuffle, so she stayed in place.

"Get that shit under control," Marco barked. In the tightly packed room, his voice stung in Isla's ears.

Juan released Luke, who took a second to find his footing and his breath again. Sweat gleamed on Juan's face, which had turned red from the effort. He panted for breath and lowered himself into a stance like a wrestler, his hands curled like claws. Behind him, Carlotta reached for her husband but fell short, only grabbing a piece of his pant leg.

MJ took three quick steps forward, the gun already out and rising. He placed it against Juan's temple and fired.

The commotion stopped. Juan's body crumpled and fell to utter silence. A beat passed as the sound of the gunshot faded, the reality of what happened sunk in, and MJ turned to point the gun at the others.

Carlotta let out a scream. Hot tears built in Isla's eyes.

"Put that shit away," Marco commanded. MJ lowered the gun, but still held it.

Luke stared at the crumpled body on the floor. "What did you do?"

"Get the rest out of here," Marco demanded.

"What did you do?"

"Move. Now!"

MJ stuck the gun in his waistband and beckoned the others. Two at a time, they moved forward, the women crying, the men lifting their hands in surrender.

Isla noticed Deepti's eyes scanning and looking for an opening. She put a hand on her arm, a warning. She felt Deepti's muscles tense and then release under her grip. She knew Isla was right. Now was not the time to resist. Juan found out the hard way.

Three rows of two stood by the door. Isla and Deepti, still in shock, hung back against the wall. Marco pointed Luke at Carlotta. "Get her."

Luke bent down to grab her arm again. She had taken her husband's hand in hers. She held it and stroked the skin with her other hand. Her lips were moving like she may have been singing a song to him. Luke didn't pull her away just yet.

MJ looked at the girls. "Get in line."

"Hang on," Marco said, trying to take command of the situation. "Leave them here."

"What for?"

"Because you gotta ditch that body."

MJ looked to Luke, but Luke had no answers for him.

"I'm sure as shit not gonna do it," Marco said. "Are you?"

Luke wouldn't even look at Juan's body. MJ glanced down at it briefly, but had to look away from the growing pool of blood around his head.

"Make them do it?" he said.

"Yeah. The mouthy one. Maybe teach her a little respect."

Deepti refused to meet Marco's eye.

Luke stood, pulling Carlotta up with him. She whimpered when Juan's lifeless hand fell from hers. Her mouth opened, but no scream came out, only a breath raspy with pain. Luke placed Carlotta at the end of the line, pointedly turning his back on the dead body. "Let's just get them out of here and then figure it out."

Like a military formation, the twin rows of captives marched out, and the door was slammed home behind them.

Isla and Deepti were now locked inside with a dead man.

"Holy shit," Deepti said.

"They killed him."

"Yeah, they did."

Isla held a picture in her mind of Marta standing with their parents. She knew then she might never see them again. Deported or dead. Tears fell down her cheeks as she cried for Juan, for Marta, for herself.

TWO

Carter couldn't see the Golden Gate, but they'd arrived in San Francisco. Larry parked his truck in front of a row of industrial warehouses, each the size of a football stadium.

"If you wait for them to offload, I can drop you at a rental place," he said.

"That's okay," Carter said. "We can take a cab."

He and Ivana had both taken advantage of the showers at the truck stop in Wyoming, as well as purchasing some new clothing, even when the only options were t-shirts, Wrangler jeans and Carhart jackets. Carter's shirt had the Peterbilt trucks logo on it, and Ivana's said ROCKY MOUNTAIN HIGH with an illustration of a row of peaks topped with snow. Carter suspected the implication might be that the snow was cocaine, but he didn't tell her that when they bought them.

"I can't thank you enough," Carter said.

"Nah, nothing to it."

Ivana held tight to Chester's leash. "I can't believe you drove straight through."

"It's nothing. I made it from Austin to Orlando in one run once. It's what we do."

Carter shook Larry's hand. "Well, we'd have been screwed without you."

"Will you do me a favor?" Larry said. "Take my number and give me a call to tell me how things turn out with this gal who's missing. I'm invested now."

"Sure thing."

They traded info, Larry gave Chester a scratch on the ears, and bid farewell.

They rented a navy blue compact car, and Ivana called Katie to get the address to enter in the GPS. The route said another four hours south along the coast.

As he returned to the car carrying a bag filled with bottled water and protein bars, Carter felt his midsection tighten. Ivana noticed his distress.

"Are you okay?"

Before he could brush off her concern, a sharp stab of pain sliced through him from his belly to his spine. He nearly dropped the bag. He knew the reason. Like when you hold off a cold during a busy time only to get sick your first day of vacation. In the cool California air, he let himself relax a little. His disease charged through the open door.

"Maybe I should drive," Ivana said.

"Yeah."

Carter folded himself into the passenger seat and waited for the pain to fade, which had been taking longer these days. He kept his grunting and groaning down so he didn't scare Ivana, but he was grateful for the cool glass of the window to lean on as she turned the rental car south and drove them out of the Bay Area.

He caught his reflection in the side mirror. A withered old man, deep lines, and red-veined eyes. He'd aged more in the past six months than in his previous seventy-two years. The disease, or his actions? A sickness eating at him from the inside out would tear him down and make him a thinning husk of who he used to be, but the same could be said for the crushing weight of leaving corpses in his wake. The life of a killer carved creases in his face like they'd been put there by knives. Self-inflicted wounds.

He saw nothing of the dramatic coastline down near Monterey, missed all of Carmel-By-The-Sea, and was asleep for the winding coastal road through Big Sur.

Ivana wished she could enjoy the scenery more, thrill to the dramatic coastal views like she starred in a car commercial or the opening credits to a rom-com, but this was no vacation. The lure of seeing her daughter after so long pulled her along the twisted highway and made the time drag. Every turn of the road may have revealed another stunning vista, but it was also a roadblock to seeing Katie.

Marta sat on the couch watching TV and munching from a bowl of chips. Bree listened to her chew and questioned whether they should get her some fruit or a healthier snack.

Katie came in from the bedroom with her phone in hand.

"They'll be here in a few hours."

"Man, I wish they'd flown," Bree said.

"I know. But they're almost here."

"Then what?"

"Then we see what Carter wants to do, and we help him."

Bree looked toward Marta again, the girl oblivious to anything but her show.

"I hope he can do something."

Katie nodded slowly. "If he can't?"

Bree shrugged. "I don't know. Child protective services? I mean, we can't keep her."

"I wish we could."

"But that's crazy."

"I know. I just want to help."

"We are helping. Or we will. We'll help Carter do whatever he needs to. We'll get Isla back. Hopefully, her parents will be back soon. We can keep her until then. As long as it takes."

Katie leaned back in her chair and ran both hands down over her face. "Damn. This world."

"I know, right?"

Katie took her hands away and looked at Bree. "In a way, it's good to know we're not the only ones with a fucked up childhood."

"Yeah, but, I don't wish that on anyone else."

"I know. But just think of it like we're trying to save someone. Not trying to…" Katie ran a single finger along her throat. Bree knew what she meant. It was the first time either one had really mentioned what happened back in Minnesota, and even then, she couldn't say the words out loud.

Bree quickly got off the subject. "A few hours, you said?"

"Yeah. They're south of Big Sur now. We'll figure it out. Don't worry."

Both of them sat watching Marta and worrying.

For a half hour the pool of blood grew, then stopped, then turned dark and viscous. Isla found it hard not to look. Deepti, for once, said nothing.

"Why do they need us for this?" Isla asked.

"To protect them," Deepti said. "Make us complicit."

"I don't get it."

"Maybe they're just scared assholes who can't do their own dirty work."

Somehow that made more sense to Isla.

* * *

MJ still held the gun.

"Will you put that fucking thing down?" Luke said.

"I don't know why Marco didn't just take all of them. Plus the body."

"You think he wants to deal with that? This is your fuck up, dude."

"Yeah, well." The air came out of MJ's argument. He kept seeing the shot go into the old man's head, accompanied by the sound. He'd fired a gun before, plenty of times. Never to kill someone. The shot had been so much louder. "I don't know why we have to listen to him on everything."

Luke got tired of waiting. He took the gun from MJ's hand and set it on the kitchen table. "Because he's the guy who knows the guy who gets us paid, that's why. And none of this would be an issue if you didn't go and fucking kill that guy."

"He was attacking you."

"Can we just get him out of my house?"

Luke led the way out the front door to the garage, and the heavy padlocks sealing the door.

"Why do we need them?" MJ asked.

"They've seen us, right? And these two keep saying they're legals. If we get them tied up in this, then we have leverage. We go down, so do they. Get me?"

"Leverage."

"Yeah. Plus, do you want to be digging a big-ass hole in the ground?"

Luke slid the door open. MJ unfolded the tarp.

"Ok, ladies." Luke clapped his hands once. "Here's how this is gonna go."

* * *

Over an hour along twisty roads climbing higher into the hills had made Isla nauseous. The blindfold didn't help. She was disoriented, and she kept slipping off the narrow seat in the back of the van when they went around sharp turns. She'd bumped up against the tarp-wrapped body several times. That brought the nausea to the forefront.

"I swear I'm gonna be sick," she said.

"How far are we going?" Deepti asked nobody.

The van had no windows, so they didn't understand why they needed the blindfolds, but they went easily with the two men after what they'd seen MJ do. Isla knew as long as she was alive, she had a chance to see Marta again. She also knew that if they'd killed once, a second would come much easier. She and Deepti had briefly talked about the idea that once the body was buried, they'd be right after it into the hole. This entire trip could be nothing more than a death march. But they put it out of their minds as too awful to think about. Plus, it would mean missing out on the bounty money for Luke and MJ, and it was easy to see money as the big motivator for these two. That and their misguided notion of cleaning up the streets of illegals, which neither woman was.

Finally, the van came to a stop. They could tell they had left pavement several miles back. When the door slid open, Isla smelled pine.

"Out," Luke said.

Their hands still zip-tied, the women were sat down against the front tires of the van while Luke and MJ removed the tarp from the back. Heat from the tires and the engine warmed their backs while the cold ground beneath them sucked it away instantly. Crunching feet over a bed of dried pine needles approached, and then the world went bright.

Isla reached up to shield her eyes now that the blindfold was off. They were in a forest. Quiet, no traffic sounds. No voices or airplanes overhead.

"Okay, dig."

Two shovels were thrown at their feet. Luke and MJ backed away from the potential weapons. Luke had a gun now. MJ's had vanished.

"You gonna take these off?" Deepti asked, lifting her bound hands, which had been switched in front of her at least. "Gonna be hard to dig with them on."

"You'll manage," MJ said. "Sorry to kill your plans." He smiled, knowing what she was plotting behind her eyes. She spotted a can of pepper spray clipped to his belt.

"You ought to be sorry for killing Juan."

Deepti stood, taking the shovel with her. Both men were on high alert for her to attack or to run. She liked seeing that they feared her.

"Where?" Isla asked.

"Anywhere you like," Luke said.

Isla scanned the woods for any sign of life. She saw none. Plans in her head for making a run for it were tabled. She had no desire to attack with the shovels, though she assumed Deepti would be making her own plans for how to get close enough to the men to make a swing at them.

"Let's just get this done," Isla said quietly to her partner.

"I wish I could tell if we were digging this for him or for ourselves."

Isla's nausea came flooding back. "Oh, God."

She bent over and vomited.

"What the hell is that?" MJ said.

"Car sick," Deepti explained.

"Just start digging."

With their hands tied, it was slow going. After a full hour, they'd made it down about eight inches. The hole was roughly the size of the body, but not nearly deep enough. *But who would ever find it out here?* Isla thought.

They had to be fairly close to a road if the van could get up here, but it was clearly not a well-traveled area. No hikers or campers would come by and trip over the body. And if they did, there was nothing to link Juan to the men and the prison cell at Luke's house.

Isla considered the act of digging as a way to keep her alive for a little while longer. As she dug, she considered of the fate the others were facing at the ICE facility. Had any of them already been loaded onto planes bound for a country they'd never seen before?

Deepti set the tip of the shovel into the ground and leaned on it.

"Got any water?"

Luke and MJ exchanged a dumbfounded look.

"You seriously didn't pack any?" she asked.

"We'll stop on the way back," Luke said.

"How much deeper you want us to go? The ground is getting harder the deeper down we get."

Luke checked his watch. He leaned forward to get a look at the hole, but couldn't see much. He stepped up to the edge and frowned.

"Gotta go deeper than–"

Deepti swung her shovel. She yelped through gritted teeth as she launched a wide arc at his head. Luke ducked and threw up one arm, dropping his gun in the process. The shovel banged off his shoulder, and Deepti lost her balance. She lunged forward with one leg to steady herself, and her foot slid into the hole.

MJ charged toward the shallow hole, bending to scoop the gun off the ground and holding it out ahead of him like a flashlight.

"No, no, no," Isla said. She let go of her shovel and stepped down into the hole, putting herself between Deepti and MJ, her back to the gun and her body curled over Deepti like branches on a willow tree.

"What was that shit, huh?" MJ asked.

Deepti had gone down to one knee and let her head hang low, expecting the shot to come any second.

"Don't," Isla said. "Just don't."

"I'm alright," Luke said. He rolled out his shoulder.

MJ seethed, tiny balls of white froth gathered at the corners of his mouth.

"I'm okay," Luke said again. He stepped forward with the palm of his hand up and flat, asking for the gun. "Hey, man. Give it here." MJ saw him working to keep the calm, but kept the gun extended.

"You just gonna take that shit?"

"It's okay. She's not gonna do it again."

Luke stared into the hole until Deepti looked up. She found his eyes and nodded.

"You're not, right?" Isla asked. Deepti nodded to her as well. Isla slowly unfolded her body and stood straight. The depth of the hole barely reached over her ankles.

With a strangled curse clenched between gritted teeth, MJ handed over the gun into Luke's outstretched hand. Luke quickly tucked it into his belt.

"Fuck it," Luke said. "It's deep enough."

He instructed the women to toss the shovels a few feet away and kept his distance. He told them to grab the body and drag him in. Isla took two fists of tarp on the side with Juan's head. She could see strands of hair leaking out from the crudely wrapped tarp. Deepti held the tarp near his feet, and they lifted him a few inches off the forest floor. Isla walked backward, but only made it a few steps before she let the tarp slide from her grip. They decided to drag him the rest of the way around the side of the van and into the hole. They adjusted as best they could, and he fit lengthwise, but the blue tarp bulged out of the hole and made a small mound.

"Cover him up," Luke said. He stayed back while they picked up the shovels again and threw the loose dirt and pine needles over the lump of blue.

To speed things up, MJ snapped off a few low branches from the trees and threw them on top of the highest spots. In ten minutes, they had him covered enough, but with a thin layer that would be whisked away in the first breeze that came down the hills and through the forest.

They all wanted to get home. None more so than Luke.

"It's fine," he said. "Good enough."

He knew there was no connection between them and the older Mexican man in the ground, even if someone did find him. Since he was undocumented, he might go unidentified anyway. No dental records, no fingerprints on file somewhere in Washington. NO telling where he came from south of the border. If anyone had been determined, surely somebody left some microscopic piece of DNA evidence, but by the time Juan was found, *if* he was ever found, that would be wiped away too.

MJ gathered the shovels and put them up front in the van. Luke stood by the sliding side door while Isla climbed inside, then Deepti. He stopped her mid-step, put a tight grip on her arm, and said, "Never again, okay?"

She drew in a breath to say something insulting to his manhood, his mother, his whole family bloodline, but she could see the way Isla looked at her and wished for her to just shut up and get them out of these woods alive.

Deepti nodded slowly, then climbed the rest of the way into the van.

Ivana drove straight to Surfside Tacos. The afternoon shift had begun and Bree and Katie left Marta with Mrs. Borgeson while they both waited on late lunchers and early diners.

Katie squealed and ran outside when she realized who was inside the car that pulled to the curb.

Carter eased himself out of the passenger seat, nervous that elongating his body would set off more cramps and pains in his gut, but he managed without any pain. Chester sat up and yawned.

The air had a cool breeze to it and an unfamiliar smell. Salt? The ocean lay only three blocks West of where they stood. The beachside business district where they were looked like it had been copied and pasted from a Mexican village in Baja. Low sand-colored adobe buildings, palm trees reaching high into the breeze, and swaying as if to a reggae beat. Everything was open-air, not built for huddling against the cold like Minnesota had been. Even this far from the beach, Carter noticed sand on the ground.

Chester climbed down from the backseat, and Carter took him for a pee against a palm tree. He needed a bathroom himself.

He could hear Ivana and Katie crying and chattering in Spanish. They clung to each other like a gust of wind might carry one away if they let go.

Bree came out the front door of the taco shop, under the angled surfboard hung over the entry with SURFSIDE TACOS airbrushed on it. She smiled at Carter, but he knew she was likely smiling at Chester. Her hair had gotten a little longer, a little lighter in the sun. She was still pale in a way that said she would never be taken for a local.

"Thanks for coming," she said.

"We should have flown," Carter said.

"Whatever. You're here now."

Chester sniffed and smelled something familiar on her. His tail swung and stirred the air more than the onshore current. Bree bent down and scratched at Chester, letting him push his head into hers and make humming noises in the back of his throat. The white on his muzzle reminded her of a dusting of snow back home.

"Come on in," she said. "You hungry?"

Katie's table got ignored as she and Ivana held hands and traded stories. Carter visited the restroom where it hurt to pee, and then told Bree to bring him whatever she knew he would like from the kitchen. They let Chester stay inside, and he laid out under the stools at the counter that was made from an old longboard coated in epoxy.

Orlando came from the kitchen and set down a plate of three tacos in front of Carter, each with a different meat. He extended a hand and introduced himself.

"This your place?" Carter asked.

"No. My cousins. My aunt owned it, and she passed it down to them when she died. I just work here and kinda act as manager. But it really runs itself."

"Manager at your age. Not too bad."

"They had to hire me. Family, y'know."

"Don't sell yourself short. Clearly, you know how to hire waitresses."

Orlando smiled and looked reflexively at Katie. He couldn't hide that he was nervous to meet Ivana. He smoothed back his hair and subtly checked his breath by breathing into his hand and sniffing quickly.

When Katie introduced him, her mother finally let go of her hand and shook his.

"I see where Katie gets her beauty from," Orlando said, properly rehearsed but still sincere. "What can I bring you to eat?"

Ivana looked at Carter's taco plate and nodded approval. "Whatever you like." Orlando dipped back into the kitchen to tell the two cooks to make their best.

"Good," Carter said between bites. "Spicy," he said after he swallowed.

"That's the pork," Bree said. "I'll get you a horchata."

In between lunch and dinner, the place was nearly empty, so Bree and Katie had time to sit and give them all they knew about Isla and where things stood, which was exactly nowhere beyond when Bree wrote the letter.

"I'm worried she's already been deported."

"We'll figure it out," Carter said. He hadn't arrived with a real idea of what to do, but getting there had been more complicated than he wanted, and he needed to know the lay of the land to make any kind of plan at all.

Ivana had made her way back into the kitchen, drawn by habit and the smells. Orlando came out and said to Bree, "She's teaching them how to make some kind of sauce."

"They could do worse," Carter said.

Orlando set down a plate of shredded beef for Chester.

"You've got a friend for life," Carter said.

"He's sweet."

"Bree tells me you know all about this."

Orlando crossed his arms. "Yeah. It sucks, man. These ICE guys, they're really making a mess of things around here. And they don't give a shit if you're an actual citizen or not. Isla, she's not illegal. It's bullshit, man."

"Agreed. So, hey, I didn't want to ask the girls because I knew they wouldn't be able to help, but maybe you can."

Orlando straightened his spine, seeing an opportunity to impress Katie. Carter lowered his voice to speak in confidence.

"Step one for me out here, I'm gonna need to get a gun."

Carter could see the request land on Orlando. The hesitation and the debate were obvious behind his eyes. He gave a quick glance back to the kitchen.

"I can't get you one," he said. "But I might know someone who can."

"Good man," Carter said.

Ivana came out of the kitchen, trailed by the two cooks, each one talking rapidly in Spanish. Ivana held a plate, still steaming, and had somehow put on an apron as if she worked there. The two cooks, both skinny men in all white, which offset their dark tanned skin, each excitedly offered Orlando a taste of the new recipe they'd been taught.

He dipped a tortilla in the dark sauce and scooped some meat to go with it. When he put it in his mouth, his eyes went wide, and his face brightened.

"Oh my God," he mumbled with a full mouth.

"I told you," Katie said. "She's the best."

Carter smelled Chester up to his usual tricks, and he had to announce that it was the dog, not him, who had passed gas, but that it was a compliment to the chefs in Chester's world.

"Maybe I'd better take him out."

Orlando agreed that was a good idea. He didn't need any emergency cleanup in his restaurant. Once Chester had been leashed up and Carter shoved the last bite of tacos in his mouth, they headed outside.

Orlando touched Katie lightly on her arm. "Can I ask you something?"

"Sure. What?"

Orlando nodded his head to the corner and walked to where nobody could overhear. Katie followed, intrigued and a little worried.

"What's wrong?"

"Nothing," he assured her. "It's just…how well do you know this guy?"

"Carter? Really well. Why?"

"It's just weird to come all this way to help out someone he doesn't even know. And he, like, asked me to help him a little. Like, get him something. I just don't know if I want to for some guy I just met."

Katie crossed her arms, threw out a hip to one side, and gave Orlando a mix of a pout and a scowl.

"Whatever it is, you get it. Whatever he needs, you do it. Understand? I owe him everything. Like, literally my life. So you do what he says, and you don't ask why, okay?"

Orlando felt like he'd been admonished by a school principal. "Yes. Yeah, okay. Sorry."

"Whatever it is," she repeated.

"Ok, I get it. Yes."

"Good." She nodded once at him, but kept the hard look on her face.

"Why don't you two knock off for the night," Orlando said. "Yeah, I can handle the tables on a weeknight. You got a lot to catch up on."

Her scowl went away, and she broke into a wide grin instantly. "Aww. You're the best," Katie said, and she leaned in to kiss his cheek. Orlando blushed as Katie went to tell Bree their shift was over.

"I don't get it, why not?"

Luke scowled and gripped the phone white-knuckle-tight in his hand. MJ had to watch silently and infer what he could from only one half of the conversation. He could tell things weren't good.

"It's bullshit," Luke said. He stayed quiet for a long while, his face falling. MJ knew he was getting an earful from Marco for being insubordinate. Ten years retired from the military, and Marco still treated everyone around him like he was their drill sergeant.

Luke finally hung up.

"Well?" MJ asked.

"They won't pay us. Wasn't a full load."

"What?"

"That's what he said. Anything short of ten, they won't pay out. We owe them three."

"What a crock of shit."

"That's what I said."

Helpless to do anything against a government who wouldn't pay up, the two men stood in the living room and stared at the carpet. Luke had quit his job, which hadn't paid much, to go full-time into the bounty business once Marco sold him on it. Things were lean and about to get leaner.

"It's a government contract, dude. Pays way more than construction shit."

It was true. He could help restore America to its once-former glory and make bank off the payments. But if he didn't actually get paid...

The garage conversion wasn't cheap. He did most of the work himself, but just the outlay for supplies had drained what savings he had. Retrofitting the van hadn't been free, either. Luke was broke.

"Did they say how long?"

"Until we deliver three more," Luke said. "Then we can get paid for that batch of ten. Then we gotta round up ten more."

"Shit, man."

"This is getting more complicated than I planned."

"If those two bitches…"

Admitting he needed money would make him seem weak to MJ, something Luke didn't want to do. Not that MJ had any money of his own, but the younger man saw weakness as a signal to pounce. To dethrone the King. And Luke liked running the show. The whole thing with Juan was exactly why MJ should never be in charge. Too young, too hotheaded, too impulsive.

"We need some income. It's gonna take time and resources to round up more."

"So what do we do?"

Luke hated to, but he said, "You had a stupid idea a while ago."

MJ pulled his shoulders back, insulted.

"Maybe it wasn't so stupid," Luke said. MJ relaxed.

"Which idea?"

"The bank."

MJ was never short of dumb ideas. He threw them out like he was feeding birds in the park, scattering half-thought-out plans and seeing if anyone picked at them. Luke had rejected his idea outright at first, but it stuck with him the smaller the numbers on his bank account got. And now that they had used the women for this other distasteful task, he gave it some real consideration.

The idea was to use the people they held in custody to go get them some extra cash. Drive them to a bank, send them in with a note and a threat, have them walk out with some money. If anything went wrong, Luke and MJ could simply walk away. Let them take the fall. When it was reported in the news, it would be an immigrant who had robbed the bank, furthering the call to get them out of the country. A win-win. The White House would be proud. Rule-bending for the right reason had been a major lesson the administration had taught Luke. When you're doing the right thing, ultimately then the smaller, insignificant rules didn't apply.

He pitched the idea back to MJ.

"Fuck yeah, dude. Let's do it."

"Okay, but hey, we gotta do it right. Don't draw attention. Nothing goes sideways. No fucking guns."

"How the hell you gonna rob a bank without guns?"

"You make them *think* we have guns. But you and me, we won't even be inside. No risk, high reward."

"Okay. Whatever you say."

Banks were closed already for the day. It would have to be tomorrow. Plenty of time for Luke to come up with a better idea, but right then, he had none.

The apartment wasn't made to accommodate five people. Marta still had Bree's bedroom. Ivana and Katie shared hers and had gone inside to talk and catch up on everything Ivana had missed. Bree set Carter up on the couch with a pillow, a sheet, and a blanket that was too small. She had gotten used to the makeshift setup on the floor of her room, so she could be there if Marta needed anything. She'd been surprised at her blooming maternal side since she never got anything resembling a lesson in motherhood from her own mom.

"This will do fine for me, thanks," Carter said and then gestured to Chester, already snoring on the floor. "And you know this one can sleep anywhere."

"I didn't know who else to call or what else to do," Bree said.

"It's okay. I'm glad you could call me for help."

"I just…after last time, I thought maybe I'd left all that behind, y'know? Like maybe I'd already had my fill of bad stuff."

"Not the way the world works, I'm afraid."

Bree sat on the floor and ran her hand along Chester's coat.

"I'm figuring that out, I guess. The world is kinda unfixable."

"It's not up to you or me to fix it. All we can do is worry about our little corner, make that the best it can be."

"I think maybe I thought coming out here would change things. Like the sunshine would kill the infection, y'know?"

"If you've got sun, you've also got shadows."

Bree sat with his words rolling around her head, running her hand along Chester's coat.

"There's just fucked up people everywhere. Like a disease you can't cure. You can treat the symptoms, but deep down, it's always there. Like herpes or something." She caught herself, blushed a little. "Oh, shit, Carter. I'm sorry."

"It's okay. You're not wrong." Bree ran a hand through her hair, squirming at her thoughtless comment. Chester lifted his head to look at her, implying that her work petting him wasn't done yet. Carter let out a raspy few chuckles. "But you're too young to be that cynical."

"You know what I've been through."

He nodded slowly. "I do. And you still picked yourself up and made a change. It's what I liked about you from the get-go. You wanted to improve your lot in life."

"I'm not sure I made my little corner any better."

"You made your life better. Look at you now. Living by the beach, you got friends, people who count on you. And you took in that little girl. You did the right thing for her. And we're gonna do the right thing for her sister."

She pushed her hair back behind her ears. "I guess when I called you, I knew it meant somebody might get hurt."

"Don't you worry about that. Our job here is to make sure that girl doesn't get hurt. And if it's too late, that anyone responsible pays for it."

"I hope it's not too late."

"So do I. But you gotta be realistic."

She set a hand on Carter's; his bones stood out through the thin skin. "Anyway, I'm glad you came."

"I mean it's just…" Isla looked for the right words. "There's not any consequences anymore, it feels like."

"None," Deepti agreed. "And no shame about anything anymore."

A single lightbulb burned overhead. The room felt empty with only the two of them there. Both still had dirt under their fingernails and stains on their pants, the smell of pine needles still clung to their clothes.

They hadn't said much on the way back from the woods. Neither wanted to relive burying a body. Neither could believe they'd done it, but the threat of a bullet is a strong motivator.

Now they were both wired from the experience and wondering if they'd be getting any food tonight. Isla sat in the strange feeling of being tired but unable to sleep, and being hungry but not wanting to eat. She and Deepti kept talking to keep from thinking about what they'd been forced to do.

"My parents came here for a better life and, I don't know, I guess they got one," Isla said. "I've never been back to where they came from, but I can't imagine it's much worse than this."

"Yeah, my grandparents came over from India. They never talked about it much. If they were alive to see this, they'd be disgusted. This isn't what they risked so much for."

"Yes, exactly. I just feel like all that land of opportunity stuff is a joke."

"But no one is laughing."

They fell into silence. The weight of their situation covered them like a blanket, threatening to smother them or at least their hope. Tomorrow was a question mark. Would they end up on a truck headed South to an ICE detention center? Stay with Luke and MJ? Which was worse?

Quietly, and unspoken between them, they slid closer until their shoulders touched. They leaned into one another, backs to the wall and hands cuffed in front of them. No dinner came, and neither one cared.

Early the next morning, Bree drove Carter to the construction site where Isla had been taken. Ivana and Katie stayed back, still talking without pause about every detail of Katie's life in California.

The site was just coming to life when they arrived. A three-story complex of apartments with retail on the ground floor, it looked to Carter about half finished. They parked on the street and walked through an open chain link gate where a large flatbed truck had just pulled in carrying a tall stack of at least fifty long metal poles, all lashed down and waiting to be unloaded.

Carter wasn't entirely sure what he expected to learn there, but he needed a place to start, and the last place Isla was seen struck him as the logical beginning.

"I'll try to find the foreman," he said as he approached the trio of mobile home offices parked on the side of the site. He knocked, and a woman answered the door. She was short and stocky with close-cropped hair and a company logo on her polo shirt.

"Yes?"

"I wonder if I can ask you a few questions about the workers who were taken from here by ICE agents last week?"

The woman scoffed. "ICE agents. They weren't no fucking ICE agents."

"How do you know that?"

She folded her arms across her chest. "Why are you asking? You a reporter or something?" She peered around Carter, looking for cameras, but saw only Bree.

Bree lifted her hand in a small wave. "We're trying to find one of the people. Isla. Do you know her?"

A flush of sadness rolled across the woman's face. "Isla. Yeah, poor kid."

"My name is Carter McCoy." He held out a hand. "We're friends of hers. We're trying to get her home."

The woman gave a skeptical eye to his outstretched hand, but then softened. "Rita. Come on in."

She pointed them to chairs in the tight space of the mobile home. Blueprints and other work plans decorated the walls while three metal desks crowded the floor.

"You say the men who took her weren't ICE?"

Rita waved a hand like the idea was ridiculous. "Nah. Never. I've seen those real ICE guys. They roll in fifteen, twenty strong. Hummers and strapped with AKs. These were the posers. Two guys. White van, no badges. But that's as official as you need these days. There's more and more of them."

"Have you seen them before?"

"Those guys specifically? No. Seen the type, though. And I've heard from other sites. At least three of our sites have been hit now. It's bullshit."

Carter crossed a leg over his knee. "I guess the big question is, do you have any idea where they might have taken her?"

"No, I don't. You know there were others, right? You gonna get them all back?"

"If we can."

"And you're, what? Some kind of lawman? Private security?"

"Concerned citizen."

Rita gave Carter a strained grin like he'd told a bad joke. "Good luck, buddy."

"Can you describe the van?" Bree asked.

"White. Plain. Shitty and old."

He didn't expect to get much, so he wasn't entirely disappointed. He knew there would be a hard road ahead. He tried to remember detective movies he'd seen over the years for a good question to ask as a follow-up.

"Can you describe the men you saw?"

"White. Plain. Shitty, but not too old."

Carter pursed his lips and nodded slowly. He'd gotten all he was going to get from Rita. "Do you mind if we ask around with some of your other workers?"

"I don't want you to freak anyone out. Everyone's a little on edge."

"Do you have a lot of illegals working here?"

"You'll never hear me say it. And if we did, they stopped reporting for shifts. We're about twenty percent down on our crew, now that they know it's a target."

"Sorry to hear that."

"Sorry? Why? Did you vote for him?"

Carter smiled and shook his head. "Thanks for your help."

He and Bree stepped out into a worksite that felt sluggish and nearly empty. If the second half of the building were to be finished any time soon, they'd need to pick up the pace. Hard to do when your workers are afraid to come to work.

Carter spotted a man mixing concrete in a small tumbler the size of an industrial washing machine. He scooped cement mix in with a shovel and turned on a hose to wet it down.

He walked close by and waved a hand. "Hiya."

The worker lifted his chin in greeting, but didn't turn off the water.

"Mind if I ask you a few questions?"

The man clenched like a fist, suspicion and fear tightening his whole body like he might run or just as likely, attack.

"We're not police," Bree said. "Or immigration."

"Hey!"

An angry voice barked at them from behind. Carter turned to see a man with a heavy gut in a short-sleeved shirt and wide tie marching in loafers across the dusty ground. He'd just parked his pickup truck, a tall Ford Raptor, the great-grandson of Carter's truck. If Carter had been a middleweight prize fighter, the Raptor was a bodybuilder. Thick and slow, long on show and short on utility. And about eighty grand.

"This is a hardhat zone, asshole. You can't be here."

Carter lifted his hands to his shoulders. "Sorry. Didn't know." He didn't mention that this man, clearly some sort of boss, also wasn't wearing a hard hat.

"Get the hell off my job site. Who the hell are you, anyway?"

"Just looking for someone. We'll go."

The boss didn't let up, even as Carter and Bree walked past him toward the open gate.

"You don't just walk in here; this is private property. You get hurt, it isn't my fault. You can't sue me."

"We're not trying to sue anyone," Carter said. He stopped and faced the man. "But if this is private property, did the men who took your workers last week have a warrant?"

"Who?"

"You had several workers abducted last week by men who claimed to be ICE agents."

"I cooperate fully with any government agency. I run a legit site."

"So the people who were taken weren't here illegally?"

The boss man's neck had gone red, and it crept up to his face, a kettle on the boil. "If I had anyone here lying on their application and trying to pull a fast one, then they got what they deserved. If it were up to me, take 'em all. Give me all Americans who can do the job. You get better work, and you keep the money here, not shipped off down to Mexico or some shit."

Carter kept his voice calm and level. Midwest nice. "But Isla wasn't illegal. She's a U.S. citizen."

"That's for them to figure out. People come in here all the time with fake documents. I can't police that shit. Goddamn cartels are behind it."

Carter looked beyond the boss to the man filling the cement mixer. If looks could kill, he would have bored holes through the boss man's back. Each stab of the shovel into the cement mix wanted to be into the boss's neck instead.

"Sorry to bother you," Carter said. "We'll go."

"Goddamn right you will." The boss ran a hand over his head, sweat beading there from his tantrum. He loosened his tie. He faced the lone worker. "Watch that hose!"

Water had begun to pour out of the mixer as the worker had been distracted by the confrontation in front of him. The boss stalked closer and started berating him.

"Maybe they ought to have taken you. Goddamn amateur. I'd fire your ass, but I can't afford to lose anyone else. Fix this shit."

As Carter and Bree hurried past the Raptor parked next to the flatbed loaded with poles, he could see Rita watching from the window of the mobile home and shaking her head in disgust. Carter paused, hidden by the trucks and already forgotten by the boss man, who had a new focus for his righteous anger.

"You still carry your knife?"

Bree nodded and pulled it from her pocket. Carter unfolded the blade and stepped closer to the flatbed. He found the heavy nylon straps holding down the load of poles. He dragged the blade across the strap. It began to split. He repeated the action, and one strap split with a pop. He moved down the long metal tube; each one had to be fifteen feet long and around six inches in diameter. He got the knife under the second strap and sliced up and across. The nylon split and the weight of the pipes, all rolling at once, finished the job without a second swipe of the blade.

He grabbed Bree's hand and hurried away as a full ton of metal pipes cascaded down onto the Raptor. He'd never heard a louder sound, and he'd seen The Who once in '77. By the time they reached the open gate, the pipes had all fallen, and the sound began to fade, only to be replaced by the shouting of the boss man as he circled his truck in ruins.

Bree couldn't help giggling as they ran.

"Do you miss him ever?"

Ivana knew who Katie meant. Her husband, Eddie. Katie's father. They'd covered all the good news. The giddy joy of seeing each other again had subsided, and now Katie could ask some things that had been on her mind that she couldn't say to anyone else.

"I wouldn't say miss him," Ivana said. "Every day, I missed a version of him I never knew. A promise he made that he never fulfilled." Ivana picked at a thread on her skirt.

"I don't miss him a goddamn bit."

Ivana almost chided her daughter not to say such things about her father, but she kept quiet. Eddie would not redeem himself in death. The things he did would never stay buried with him. They lived on in the scars on these two women.

"I wasn't sure if you'd come," Katie said. "I mean, we only really asked Carter."

Ivana reached up and ran a hand along her daughter's hair. "Of course I would come. I wasn't going to miss the chance to see you again."

"Is it safe back home? I mean, like, nobody is gonna ask questions about…?"

"No, no. That's all done. Finished."

Katie exhaled, letting go of a little piece of the past she'd been holding. "And now this shit. It's like, no matter what you do, you can't escape it, right? Assholes everywhere."

Her father's mouth. One thing she would always keep from him.

"We will do our best to make things right," Ivana said.

"If we can. I just can't help feeling, like, helpless, y'know?"
"I know. I know it well."
Ivana leaned into Katie and rested her head on her shoulder.

Luke shifted his eyes from the front of the bank to the clock on the dashboard of the van. Three minutes until opening. The women were in back with their instructions and a note for each of them threatening that they had a gun and accomplices and to put all the cash in a bag.

When Luke explained the plan to Isla and Deepti that morning, they both listened in stunned silence.

"Do you understand?" he asked.

"You want us to rob a bank?" Deepti asked.

"Yeah. Kinda."

She had no angry or sarcastic comeback for him.

In the back of the van, the women discussed what to do. After seeing a man gunned down in front of them, they didn't want to give MJ another excuse to do the same.

"It means they need us," Isla said.

"Yeah, need us to take the risk. If we get shot or arrested, they still get away. I can describe them, but I still don't know where the house is. I can't see shit any time we're in this van. And then there's that dead body stuff. That makes us accomplices."

"But we had to, or they'd kill us." Isla's stomach flipped at hearing how close that sounded to 'just following orders'.

"You try explaining that. Look at us. The goddamn Supreme Court said they could pull people off the street just for looking any shade but white. You think anyone is gonna take our word for it over theirs? Maybe when Barack was President, but not now."

A portly man in a dark blue suit came to the glass front door of the bank and unlocked it. Luke tapped MJ with the back of his hand.

"Let's go."

Bright morning light blasted into the back of the van when the door slid open.

"You got your notes?"

The women nodded.

"You know what to do?"

They nodded again.

MJ leaned into the open door. He eased the butt end of the gun out from under his jacket. "You know not to fuck around?"

They nodded a third time.

"Then let's go."

Luke held the glass door for them. "You stay here. Nobody comes in," he told MJ. "And don't shoot anybody."

He followed Isla and Deepti inside, the first customers of the day. They each held their handwritten note in their zip-tied hands, crossed in front of them. Luke parked himself at the small stand with deposit slips and a pen on a chain. He kept his face tilted down, away from any cameras. He shooed them away toward the tellers.

Isla and Deepti split up after one last look for encouragement. They'd been instructed not to speak. Merely hand over the note and wait. The whole thing should be over in three to five minutes.

Isla placed her note on the dark faux-stone counter and slid it forward under the safety partition. The teller was a middle-aged woman still setting up for the morning. The coffee cup to the side of her cash drawer steamed with a fresh brew. She'd been engrossed in her setup and hadn't noticed Isla's bound wrists.

"Good morning," the teller said by rote. "How may I help you?"

She lifted the note and read it, looked at Isla, then read it again.

"Are you serious?"

Isla nodded.

Two windows down, Deepti kept her hands up on the counter and drummed her fingers, trying to get the teller to notice the zip-ties. "Holy shit," her teller said.

The note had instructions on which bills to collect (no singles) and threats about not pushing any alarms, silent or otherwise.

Luke hung by the deposit slip station and twirled the chain from the pen around his finger with nervous energy, hoping he hadn't made a stupid choice to take MJ's idea on, and also wondering how this would help in making America great again. His life had been rolling along like a car left in neutral at the top of a hill lately. Careening out of his control toward an uncertain end.

* * *

Outside, a man approached the bank dressed in business casual. MJ had seen him turn the corner at the end of the block. He carried a navy blue deposit bag, about the size of a woman's purse, and it bulged in the middle, quite full.

MJ stepped forward to block his way. "Bank's not open yet."

The man, skeptical, leaned around MJ to peer through the glass doors.

"I see people in there."

"Cleaning crew."

The man tucked the deposit bag up under his armpit. "Hey, what is this, a gag?"

"Come back later."

He tried to step around MJ. "It looks open to me."

MJ side-stepped and blocked him again. The man was annoyed now, but still didn't seem to suspect anything like a robbery. Just another asshole, the kind he met all day long.

"Listen, pal–"

MJ punched him in the stomach. It caught the man totally off-guard, and he buckled, wheezing for a breath that wouldn't come. MJ caught him as he fell and held him up off the ground. A man flat on his face on the sidewalk might draw attention, and they still had two minutes left.

∗ ∗ ∗

The teller in front of Isla wouldn't look at her at all. The teller in front of Deepti never took her eyes off her. She fumbled getting the stacks of cash into the bag. The note had the threat of armed gunmen hiding and blocking the entrance. The teller complied dutifully, following the bank's policy of not resisting. They'd trained for this, but that had been one afternoon a long time ago. And being told by a corporate liaison to remain calm during a simulated robbery in a Marriott banquet room turned out to be quite different from the real thing.

Isla took the blue deposit bag when it was pushed under the Plexiglass partition, the teller still not looking up as if that were part of the instructions. Deepti's bag hung up under the pass-through, and she had to yank hard on it to get it through.

Luke kept an eye on the man in the blue suit. He sat at a desk in the far corner, typing at a computer and ignoring anything else going on inside the bank. A few simple withdrawals didn't concern him.

When both Isla and Deepti stepped away from the tellers at the same time, Luke snapped to attention. He kept his head down as they passed by him, and he fell in behind them.

Out of habit, the teller who'd helped Deepti said, "Thank you."

Luke stepped aside and pushed the women through the door. Had it really been that easy?

On the sidewalk, Luke realized it might not have been that easy at all. He didn't quite understand why MJ held onto a man who looked drunk.

"Jesus Christ."

"It's fine," MJ said. "He's fine."

"Get in the van."

MJ had to let the man go. He fell to one knee with a whimper. MJ wanted to shout at him to learn how to take a punch, but he jogged the five steps to the van, opened the side door, and took the deposit bags from Isla and Deepti as they climbed back inside. He slammed the door, sealing them in darkness again.

Luke noticed by the upward curve in the corner of his mouth the moment MJ had an idea. With the heft of the two bags in his hands, he looked at the man on the ground and the deposit bag he'd dropped. MJ swiftly moved across the sidewalk again and scooped up the third bag.

"What are you doing?" Luke asked. "Leave it."

"Could be a lot in here."

The man on the ground grabbed MJ by the ankle. He still had some fight in him. MJ tugged, but the man held on, nearly pulling MJ off his feet.

Luke hopped side to side by the front of the van, all nervous energy and wanting to get moving. "Let's go."

MJ pulled again, and the man reached out his other arm and got a two-handed grip on MJ's leg. A woman across the street craned her neck to see the fight as she walked past. MJ reached into his jacket and came out with his gun.

Luke sprinted forward. He clamped a hand on MJ's wrist and pointed the gun at the sidewalk.

"Are you fucking nuts?"

"Get him off me," MJ said.

Luke kicked the man in the chest. For the second time, his breath left him, and his grip loosened. Luke had MJ by the shoulders and pulled him away. MJ tried to get his own kick in on the man, but Luke yanked him toward the van.

"Get in."

"Stupid motherfucker."

"Just get in!"

Luke ran around the front of the van and got in the driver's side. He pulled away, thinking how he was going to justify this. For all the bleeding heart liberals crying about how ICE were carrying out illegal raids or the Executive Orders weren't in line with Presidential powers, what he had just done was a crime. No two ways about it. He'd seen plenty of justifications for crimes in recent years, and most of them made sense when it was in the best interest of the country. But this? How could he make sense of it?

Then again, what did he do? He walked into a bank, stood around, and walked out. He didn't actually *DO* anything. They did.

Of course, he was keeping the money. MJ had already opened the two bags from the women and was working on the lock from the man he punched.

Maybe once he got paid his bounties he could return the money. Drop it anonymously through the night deposit slot.

But what they were doing was the right thing. Cleaning up the streets. Making America Great Again. And the government insures banks. They wouldn't lose a dime. So, in a way, the government just paid Luke for his work in a roundabout way. It all came from the same source in the end. His tax dollars. And it wasn't a handout, like those illegals are getting. He worked hard for it.

He started to calm down, slow his breathing, and wonder how much the take was.

Orlando swung by to pick up Carter, but balked when he saw Chester.

"I didn't know you were bringing the dog, man."

Carter held tight to the leash, though Chester didn't seem eager to go anywhere without him.

"The girls are going out. Nobody can look after him. He won't bother anyone."

Orlando rolled his eyes. "Okay, whatever, man."

Chester climbed slowly into the back seat of Orlando's sun-faded Prius.

"I want you to know, man, this isn't something I normally do," Orlando said. "I don't even smoke weed, and I don't like to mess with the gang shit."

"So who's this we're seeing?"

"A cousin."

Carter nodded and eased himself into the front seat. Orlando steered them East into a grid of flat blocks with one-level stucco houses all in shades of sand colors.

"Same cousins who own the restaurant?" Carter asked.

"No, different. I got a lot of cousins."

The neighborhood wasn't like anything in Minnesota. Smaller lots. Fewer trees. Barely anything green except for the tops of the palm trees, which grew high overhead.

"Is it true nobody has basements out here?" Carter wanted to know.

"Basements? Nah, not around here, man."

"Hmm." The streets continued by in anonymous uniformity. "Earthquakes, I guess."

Orlando shrugged. He had no opinion.

In another five minutes, they parked in front of a low chain-link fence. In the driveway of the house was a card table with six men gathered around slapping dominoes down. A speaker was playing a kind of dancehall reggae mixed with *Tejano* music. The men were loud, and two of them smoked cigars. Most were in tank tops, but one was shirtless with a tattoo of the Virgin Mary covering most of his chest.

Orlando licked his lips and swallowed. "Let me talk, okay, man?" He rolled the window down a few inches so Chester would have some air and then got out.

Carter followed a few paces behind as Orlando walked into the driveway. The talk stopped, but the music played on. Everyone stared at their young cousin, then at the old man he'd brought with him.

"Hey," Orlando said. "How you doing, Chuy?"

A heavyset man in a white tank top sat centered at the card table with two dominoes in his hand. Carter assumed he was the owner of the house.

"Hey, cuz," Chuy replied.

"This is my boy, Carter."

Carter waved, but nobody returned it. "Hi, fellas."

"This is the cat who's meeting with *Payaso*?" Chuy asked.

"Yeah."

The looks Carter got were a mixture of confusion and pity. Chuy laid his dominoes face down on the table and stood. "Not here. Come with me."

Orlando waved Carter on through the crowd as Chuy led them to a detached garage. Two of the men, including the shirtless one, followed behind.

"I don't like this going down here," Chuy said.

"I know, man. I just needed a place *Payaso* knew. He's not gonna meet me someplace he don't know."

"I don't like *Payaso*, either. This is a one-time thing, cousin. One time."

"Heard," Orlando said.

Chuy bent down and lifted the garage door. It squeaked on the rollers and revealed a one-car space with a weight bench, a hanging heavy bag, and the front fenders and a hood from a classic car, but no other signs of the vehicle.

"So," Chuy said to Carter. "My boy says you're here to fuck with ICE."

"I'm here to help a girl, that's all."

"Anyone here to fuck with ICE is okay by me."

The other men nodded in agreement. "*Mierda inmigración*," the men both said at the same time.

Chuy sized Carter up, shoes to the top of his thin grey hair. "So you like, ex-military or something?"

"No, not me. Just a friend."

Chuy looked to Orlando for some explanation, but Orlando had none.

Carter didn't explain any further. The less they knew, the better. He wasn't sure he could easily explain it all anyway.

Heavy bass sounds preceded a mid-70s Buick Riviera riding very low on its shocks. It parked, blocking the driveway, and Carter could feel the bass in his chest from the garage.

The engine and the music shut off. From the passenger side emerged a man at least six foot four. Carter looked him up and down, and aside from the bright colors he wore, he noticed his shoes were impossibly large, like a pro basketball player.

Orlando tapped Carter on the shoulder. "Okay, let me talk, man."

So, Payaso had arrived.

The driver got out and waited by the car. Payaso wore a bright yellow jacket that hung down past his hips. He walked straight forward past the card table and the men there, ignoring all of them. Someone turned down the music to a low murmur. Chuy stepped out of the garage to meet him.

"*Payaso, ¿como estas? Sabes, mi primo.*"

Chuy pointed to Orlando, who gave a timid wave. Payaso gave a passing glance at Orlando and fixed on Carter.

"*¿Quién es ese?*"

"*Esto es Carter.*"

Carter picked out his name from the mess of words he didn't know and assumed introductions were being made. He extended a hand.

"Carter McCoy. Thanks for meeting with me."

Payaso regarded the hand like it was filled with shit. "Yeah, but *¿quién es él?*"

"I don't know, man," Chuy said. He took two steps back down the driveway and called out to Orlando. "This is all you, cousin."

Orlando took a breath and stepped up. *"Él es mi amigo."*

"Tu amigo, no el mío."

Carter could sense the tension. He reached into his pocket and removed the folded wad of bills. Five hundred dollars.

"I don't want to take up your time. All I want is the gun, and then we'll go."

He held out the cash the same way he held out the last bite of his cheeseburger for Chester. Payaso looked at it the same way Chester eyes that meat.

"You a cop?" Payaso asked in English.

"No. Not a cop."

"Lift up your shirt."

Checking for a wire, Carter assumed. He complied. He had nothing to hide.

Payaso didn't seem satisfied. He wanted to reach for the cash, Carter could tell, but once he did, if it was a setup, then he'd be screwed.

Orlando raised a finger like he was in a classroom asking permission to speak. "Payaso, I—"

A steel blade look cut him short.

Carter kept the money on offer, hanging in the air between them. Payaso reached into the deep pocket on the left side of his jacket. He came out with a small pistol, scuff marks on the finish showing bare metal through the black. He held it flat on his palm and bounced it slightly. He seemed to have no intention of handing it over.

Orlando began backing up, shrinking into the rear wall of the garage. His cousin moved slowly to the side, out from behind Carter and out of the line of fire.

Payaso turned the gun in his hand and held it by the grip. He could fire it now, if he wanted, and he looked like the debate raged behind his eyes. Carter held the money, but now it trembled a bit at the end of his outstretched hand. Not from fear, but from holding his arm extended for so long.

He considered trying to explain to Payaso about his condition and how the threat of a gun didn't bother him as much as it might someone else, but he figured silence was the best choice. Let this man take all the time he needed to decide what he was going to do. When that moment stretched on too long, and he felt he might drop the money, Carter said,

"If it helps, all I need it for is—"

"I don't give a fuck what you need it for. Don't want to know. If you're buying from me, it ain't good. Not exactly hard to get a gun here. But a clean one, like this? Nah, man, I don't wanna know."

"Fair enough."

From the end of the driveway, Chester barked twice. Carter was impressed if the old dog could tell Carter may be in danger. He didn't think Chester could even see that far these days. Then again, maybe he'd only seen a squirrel.

Payaso turned to see the source of the barking. "Your dog?"

"Yes. Name's Chester." Chester barked again, as if introducing himself.

Payaso turned back to Carter, a slight smile on his face now. "Coon hound?"

"That's right."

"Ever take him hunting?"

"No. He's got a hell of a nose for anything in the backyard, though."

"No doubt, no doubt. Shit, that's a good-looking dog."

"You want to see him closer?"

"Shit, yeah."

Carter nodded to Orlando. "Go ahead. Go get him."

Orlando didn't seem so sure, but the way Payaso had suddenly changed into a little boy on Christmas morning appeared to neutralize the threat. Orlando hurried down the driveway past the dominoes game, which had stopped so everyone could watch.

"For you," Carter said, wiggling the cash.

"Oh, yeah, shit." Fast as a viper strike, Payaso snatched the money from Carter's hand, and it vanished into his pocket.

As soon as Orlando opened the door, Chester bounded past him faster than he could grab the leash. He loped up the driveway, trailing the leash behind him, and made a straight line for Carter, passing under the dominoes table. He reached the old man and sniffed him up and down, making sure was okay.

"Go on," Carter said. "He loves ear scratches."

Payaso slipped off the yellow jacket and draped it over the weight bench. "Everything is in there. Pick one you want."

He turned all his focus onto Chester, who lapped up the attention. Carter picked through the pockets and ended up choosing the same scraped-up gun Payaso had been holding. It was small enough to fit in his pocket, easy enough to handle. He hoped like hell he wouldn't even have to use it.

"This is a good dog, my man."

"Don't I know it," Carter said.

Payaso looked up at him, but kept scratching Chester. "How much you want for him?"

"Oh, no. He's not for sale."

"You take the gun. No charge."

"No, thanks. He stays with me. We both got plans together."

"A shame." Payaso stood. He gave a short, two-finger salute to Chuy. "Call me." With one last pat on Chester's head, Payaso lifted his jacket off the bench, turned and walked back down the driveway, and got into the waiting Buick.

Chuy slapped Carter on the back. "You got balls, man."

"Not so much. He just had to get it out of him, I could tell. He wanted me to know who was in charge."

Orlando came out from the shadows of the garage. "Let's get the hell out of here."

Carter clicked his tongue and patted his thigh twice. Chester fell in beside him and walked back through the crowd of dominoes players to Orlando's car.

"Sorry to interrupt, gentlemen," Carter said.

Isla crumpled the empty bag of McDonald's and tossed it in the corner. Luke and MJ had stopped on the way back, the only thing that interrupted their arguing. They could hear the muffled shouting through the partition in the van, Luke berating MJ and MJ standing up for himself and spouting his gun rights under the Second Amendment.

"So, what do you think happens now?" she asked Deepti.

"Hell if I know."

"I can't believe any of this."

"It's a fucking nightmare, that's for damn sure. There's gotta be a way out."

"I don't trust the smaller one."

Isla could see Deepti's mind spinning behind her eyes. Plans for violent revenge and revolt. But both of them were helpless for the moment, but if she had her chance…

* * *

Luke sent MJ home. He let him take the sealed deposit bag he'd stolen from the businessman. Let him burn out his energy breaking into it.

He never imagined cleaning up the streets would be this complicated. Now, a man was dead, a bank robbery had taken place, they still hadn't been paid. The libtards kept spewing lies about the President having a history of not paying people, but it was all jealousy and their sick woke mind virus, Luke knew.

He took a beer from the fridge, turned Fox News on the TV, and sat down on the couch, ignoring the screen. It made for good background noise. A welcome friend who understood him, not like MJ.

Luke had been working on cultivating his male friendships. He needed like-minded people in his life. Needed masculine energy. So far, he'd struck out.

He hadn't realized how alone he was until he started actively looking for more friends. His pickup work at construction sites meant he never stayed in any one place too long, so he never formed concrete bonds with people. He didn't have the money to go out to bars every night. A weird kind of isolation and loneliness crept up on him, and now here he was, in his mid-30s, and all he wanted was someone to sit and watch the game with.

He tipped the bottle, but it came back empty. Drained already without him even noticing. He set it down and rose to get another from the fridge.

* * *

MJ drove back home, where he knew his mom would have a hot meal waiting for him. Luke had been such a pussy lately. Since the shooting, it was like MJ's balls had dropped. A new confidence came over him. He was doing it, making a difference. Putting his trigger finger where his mouth had been.

Luke didn't have the same commitment to do it. Wearing a red hat didn't make you a real part of the movement. Action did. And MJ had proved himself a man of action.

Maybe it was time to take over for Luke. Move into the driver's seat. He'd have to talk to Marco about it. They needed someone in charge of this operation who had the guts to act when the time came.

Maybe he'd outgrown this little freelance operation. Time to go fill out his application at ICE. They dropped the high school diploma requirement, so no more hurdles in his way. He could be getting paid big bucks, a pension, health care, all that shit. A real job, not like these illegals sucking at the government tit, begging for socialism.

And they'd give him a bigger, better gun. An automatic. Train him to use it. Give him a license to kill when one of the fuckers got out of line, like that stupid old bastard did.

When they witnessed him in action, saw him use all this experience to grab more than anyone else, they'd give him a fuckin' medal.

He turned up the volume on the Kid Rock radio playlist on his Spotify and wondered what Mom would have cooking for lunch today.

Carter slept with the gun under his pillow.

Orlando had dropped him off and scurried away, not even taking time to talk with Katie. Bree asked questions about how it went, and Carter laid out the basics while skipping most of the details and the whole fear of getting shot thing. The important thing was, he had a gun now and had taken a first step.

Or maybe a delay tactic.

In truth, he still didn't have much of a plan. Tomorrow would be the day to decide on a real course of action.

Chester snored away on the floor next to the couch, worn out from the car ride and his worry about the old man. Carter awoke suddenly around one a.m. He needed to pee urgently. He couldn't start the habit of wetting the bed in the middle of the night. He already felt decrepit enough, and he couldn't ignore the way those guys in the driveway, and Orlando, and maybe even Katie and Bree, looked at him. Wondering how this old man would be their savior.

He stepped over Chester and half-stumbled to the bathroom, making it just in time. Each time now, his bladder seethed with fire. His gut cramped, and he had a hard time standing. When he finally finished, he had to stay in the bathroom another ten minutes trying to stand up straight without feeling like a razor was being dragged across his stomach.

He faced the mirror, deep wrinkles and a sheen of sweat coating his face staring back at him. He ran cold water and cupped his hands, splashing his face over and over until the heat wave passed. Cramps moved from his stomach to his kidneys to his head like he fought an invisible opponent.

He stood hunched, smaller and beaten down, lower than he'd ever been. Looking at himself in the mirror, he wondered when it had gotten so bad. How had he not noticed? Even this trip had taken so much out of him, like his insides were filled with sand and it was running out of the hourglass.

Carter drank water from the tap, breathed deep through his nose and out his mouth. It neared a half hour before he emerged from the bathroom. The rest of the apartment remained quiet. He missed the sounds of the woods outside his home. The insects, the howls of animals on the hunt, the breeze moving a million pine needles at once.

The apartment was far enough away that they didn't get any ocean sounds. The only trees nearby were a few palm trees at the end of the block, and they didn't make noise like a Minnesota forest.

He walked back to the living room as quietly as he could. When he got there, he found Chester on the couch. He tried shoving him to one end, but Chester grumbled and flopped his head onto the pillow, leaving a smear of drool across the pillowcase. Carter huffed and climbed over Chester, squeezing himself between the dog and the cushions, and fell back into a fitful sleep.

Carter finished his breakfast just as Bree returned from dropping Marta off at school. Ivana couldn't help herself and made a full spread of eggs and bacon and pan-seared tomatoes for everyone.

The weight of the gun in his pocket pulled at him, daring to be ignored. He didn't think he'd ever get used to the heaviness, or the heaviness of what it meant to use a gun. He'd kept it on him since he returned from Orlando's cousin's. With a young girl in the apartment, he didn't want any accidents.

Beyond acquiring the gun, Carter hadn't had many ideas of how to track down Isla. Everyone he'd hunted in the past had been easy to find. Someone he knew, like Justin Lyons, or someone Detective DeFore had given him. Finding a missing person was beyond his capacity.

Bree had told him about her attempt to stake out the place where she knew others had been taken. He didn't have anything better, so his plan was to go there and see what he could see. But time kept ticking for Isla.

Ivana took his plate and turned on the faucet in the sink.

"No, no, let me," Carter said. "You did all the cooking."

"And used up all our eggs," Katie said.

"You don't have enough here to feed a mouse," Ivana said.

"It's not a restaurant, Mom."

"Still, you have guests."

Katie playfully scowled at her mother. Carter started washing the dishes.

"I had an idea," Ivana said. Carter shut off the water. Bree and Katie both leaned on the countertop bar that separated the kitchen from the living room.

Ivana went on with everyone listening. "You can look all you want, but we need to focus on what *they* are looking for. Bree, when you went out there, nobody was looking for you. They're looking for me."

She let it sit in the air between them, then explained. "If I go out to one of the places where they might pick people up, be like bait. Lure them in. And then you," she addressed Carter, "be waiting nearby. We catch them in the act."

"No, Mom, it's too dangerous."

"Then what's your idea?"

Ivana got back only silence from the other three. Wheels turned in all their heads, but nobody had a better idea.

Energized by her idea, Ivana went on. "Carter will be there. He will see them. He can follow them. They'll lead us right to her."

"If she's even still here and not in some detention facility," Bree said.

"If we can find where she was," Carter said, "then we can find where she is. We can go to any detention center and make inquiries. Hire a lawyer. Get her out. She's a citizen, for God's sake."

"I don't know if you've been paying attention to the news," Bree said. "But that doesn't matter much anymore."

"I think it will work," Ivana said.

Another silence settled over them as everyone tried to think of a better plan.

"I don't love it," Carter said. "But she's right. Maybe we need to build a better mousetrap, you know?"

Katie was near tears. "It's dangerous."

Ivana went and put an arm around her daughter. "I'll be safe. Carter will be there."

"We should go now, then," Carter said. "Mornings are more likely when they'd be out looking."

Ivana stood straight and smoothed her clothing. "I'm ready."

MJ agreed to leave his gun at home when they went out to get the last bodies they needed to deliver a full load to Marco. Luke had negotiated him down to a knife, but that was it. He left the gun sitting out on his desk, where he used to do homework in middle school, with no fear of it being discovered. His mother would never enter his room unannounced. MJ threatened to leave home if she ever did that. She didn't know he had no intention of leaving, even after she died, when he would inherit the house and live rent-free for life.

Luke could tell MJ had ideas of going solo, ditching Luke, and gathering his own load of ten to deliver. Fine with him. This may be the last load he did with MJ anyway. He didn't need someone so unpredictable. Things had already gotten far more complicated than he planned.

After the argument on the drive home from the bank, with the playground insults and posturing for dominance, they rode in near silence. There were a half a dozen places where they knew migrant workers waited for day work. Each time they went out, they found fewer and fewer people on the streets. A testament to how well the plan was working. Their President truly was making America Great Again, even if it did make it harder to gather bodies for the bounty. Maybe this wasn't as much of a long-term plan as Luke thought it might be.

Still beat sweating his ass off on a construction site or out in some field picking strawberries. He'd accepted long ago that he wasn't a business type. He entertained the idea of owning some store, but had no idea of what or how to do that. His high school diploma put him in a category of blue-collar worker, but to Luke, he always deserved more.

The time had come for both of them to sign up for ICE full-time. Get real badges and real authority. MJ would do well with a commander keeping him in line. Luke bristled at the idea of authority like that. He knew he wouldn't do well. Being his own boss was the way to go. Wasn't that the American dream anyway? Not taking orders from some guy your same age just because of some stripes on his uniform.

"Empty," MJ said as they passed by the parking lot outside a home improvement store. "God dammit."

"We might need to start taking this show on the road. Widen our scope."

"Let's check the other places first. I don't want to spend all day driving around creation."

Luke turned the van east, and they continued on in the quiet.

Carter parked on the far end of the lot. A single-level strip mall similar to many he'd seen since arriving in California. A liquor store, a CPA office that looked abandoned, a Mexican restaurant that was still closed, and then Ivana on the far end of the lot. They stopped when they spotted two others standing and waiting for a chance at work. A woman and a man. They stood apart from each other, not talking, so Carter assumed they didn't know each other. He let Ivana out, and she joined the trio in a separated silence.

It hadn't reached 9:30 yet, so the lot was empty of customers for the shops. Carter had a wide view of both entrances to the lot on the intersecting streets. He rolled down his window and powered off the car, figuring he might be in for a long wait. There was a decent chance they could wait all day, every day, for a week and not lure anything.

Chester sat up behind him in the backseat. He sniffed the air coming in through the open window, then got bored and lay back down.

"I promise I'll take you to the beach before we leave here."

Thin clouds floated high overhead, but the sun shone directly on the parking lot and the blacktop absorbed heat easily. A flatbed work truck turned the corner and passed by the three waiting. Carter noticed the man and woman stand straighter, anticipating, but then slumped back down when the truck passed. Ivana studied the streets around her, secretly enjoying the assignment.

Ten minutes went by, and Carter thought about taking Chester out for a bathroom break. He thought about one for himself, too. Maybe that liquor store had a restroom he could use, even if he had to buy a pack of gum or a water bottle. If things got desperate, he and Chester could both pee against a palm tree.

He reached over and took the gun from the glovebox. He set it in the cup holder. He didn't like seeing it there, even if he knew it would be best to have it close. He found a wad of napkins in the side pocket of the door from some fast-food stop they'd made on the trip out West and covered the gun.

A white van drove into the lot and made a U-turn to park near the three waiting. Carter sat up in his seat, eyes trying to make out the license plate. When the man and woman ran over to the van as if beckoned, Carter knew they were in business.

"Work? Huh? *¿Trabajo?*"

Luke stayed behind the wheel. A short man with tanned skin and a pearl-buttoned denim shirt reached MJ's passenger window first.

"*Si.*"

"Fifty bucks," MJ said. He had no intention of paying the man, but it got them into the van, at least. He'd been jealous when he watched news reports of men in full camo gear with tactical vests on, AR-15s in their hands, real badges, and ICE-branded gear. Until they could afford that stuff, they used a "free candy" method to lure immigrants like a pedophile would lure children.

MJ got out and waved the three toward the side door. Three at once would put them over the ten they needed, and it meant extra money.

The man hustled into the van. The woman hesitated.

"*¿Qué trabajo?*"

"We need workers. All kinds. Come on, fifty bucks, let's go."

After another moment of hesitation, she followed. Ivana stepped forward.

"What kind of work do you need?"

MJ gave her an annoyed look. "All kinds, C'mon."

"Do you hire a lot of women?"

Her fear was going with the wrong crew. She needed to find the people who had Isla, not waste her time getting hired by a legitimate work crew.

"Yeah, sure," MJ said.

"For what? Cleaning? Cooking?"

He rolled his eyes and leaned his head back. "Okay, fine." He reached under his shirt and took out the badge he'd gotten from a costume shop and hung on a chain around his neck.

"Ok, lady, ICE agents. Get in the van."

From inside the van, the man said in a panicked voice, *"La migra!"*

The fun of the undercover work evaporated in an instant. Ivana knew the danger as surely as if a rattlesnake and shaken its tail. It hit her, sharp and stinging like two fangs piercing her skin, that this could end very badly for her. She'd become a citizen by marriage, but now that man was dead and gone. It would take very little to fall through the cracks these days. She gave a quick glance across the lot to Carter's car, but she knew the plan was to wait until she got in and drove away so he could follow and lead them to Isla.

She took a small step back. MJ reached out a hand and took hold of her wrist.

From inside the van, the man they'd taken in rumbled forward and tried to push through. He banged against MJ as he tried for an escape, but was blocked from leaving the van. MJ spun, his right hand still holding Ivana, and elbowed the man in the gut. He tumbled back and knocked over the woman behind him. When he pushed up and made another lunge for the door, MJ had drawn his knife.

MJ swung down and plunged the knife into the man's foot, ramming the blade all the way through until it hit the floor of the van. The scream brought Luke around from the front.

"What the hell is going on?"

"He made a break for it."

"Jesus, fucking…"

Together, Luke and MJ pushed Ivana into the van. The three captives tumbled together in a pile, the man still screaming and holding his foot.

"Go, go!" Luke urged.

"Wait!" MJ said. "My knife." He pushed Luke aside and leaned in, got a firm grip on the knife, and pulled up. The man let out another, equally pained and loud scream when the knife tore from his foot. He crumpled to the floor of the van in a fetal position.

MJ leaned forward and wiped the blade of the knife on the man's pants, smearing them with his own blood. He leaned back out and slammed the door shut.

"Now we can go."

Luke scrambled around the back end of the van as MJ took his time getting in.

Carter tried to make sense of the chaos at the door of the van. He sat far enough away he couldn't tell much about what was happening, but a loud shout of pain cut across the lot, and then, like it was a nightmare of his brought to life, he saw Ivana get pulled inside.

It didn't look like she had been hurt; the screams had not been hers, but he wanted nothing more than to rush to her aid and stop this. But if he followed the plan and let things play out, they may lead him to Isla.

He put the car in gear, his heart racing. This was it; things were in motion now. The drive out here hadn't been for nothing. He *could* help. They would get her back.

The van skidded tires as it made a quick escape from the lot. Carter put his foot on the gas and felt the first cramp in his gut. The adrenaline burst came over him in a euphoric wave, but then settled back into a lightheaded haze. His car leaped from the parking spot, but his grip on the wheel loosened.

The cramp turned to fire, and he grunted. Pain ran from his ribs to his hips like a hot wire tracing the outline of his skeleton. Ahead, the van left the lot, found the street, and then made an immediate right turn. Carter accelerated across the lot.

His insides twisted and burned. He bent forward, his forehead almost resting on the steering wheel, his foot still on the gas. Behind him, Chester sat up as the car raced over the uneven pavement. Carter's vision went blurry at the edges, then dimmed. His cramps had never been this bad. The excitement, the nerves, had set something off in him.

He aimed for the curb cut into the street and found it, barely. One hand slid off the steering wheel as his vision began to go dark at the periphery. He knew he had to turn right, but his arms wouldn't obey. The rental car hit hard as one tire went over the curb. The turn never came. His eyesight became tunnel vision and then darkness. His foot slid off the gas, and his hands dropped to his lap. The car continued on across two lanes of the street, Chester up and looking out the window, along for the ride. The car banged over the curb and onto an island at the intersection, ran over a short succulent plant, and pressed the front bumper against a covered bus stop.

Carter lay still behind the wheel.

THREE

Voices called through the dark. A tarry blackness gave way to a dull orange glow of the sun through his eyelids. He opened them to see strange faces.

"I don't know, he just drifted across both lanes and went over the curb."

"Jesus, I thought he was dead."

"Did somebody call an ambulance?"

He didn't know any of the voices or the faces. He didn't know where he was or why it was so bright. He didn't know why they were talking about ambulances.

"Should we move him?

"No. But check his pulse or something."

A clammy hand took hold of his wrist. In a shock of light, it came back to him: Ivana driving away inside the van. The pain that seized his gut. His failed mission.

Carter twisted in his seat and reached for his seatbelt.

"Hey, hey, man, settle down. Ambulance will be here soon."

He looked for the street, maybe to see the van make a turn he could follow, but the only thing ahead of him were a few brown, spiky bushes and the backside of a bus stop. He'd gone off the road when he passed out. He had no idea how long he'd been out.

Carter turned to the passenger seat and expected Chester to be looking back at him with that sad expression he gave when his dinner was late. But the seat was empty.

"My dog," he said.

He could make out the face of a man in his mid-twenties leaning in the car. He'd been the owner of the clammy hand.

"Uh, yeah, dude. When we opened the door, he got out."

Carter tried to sit up to see out the window, but the belt held him in place.

"I saw it run that way." A woman in her fifties pointed to the right, but made no move to chase down Chester.

"My dog," Carter said again.

"Relax, man. The pound will pick it up. Probably."

The pain had left a hollowed-out center in his body, made deeper and more empty by his failure to follow Ivana and now losing Chester in a strange town. Chester had nothing resembling survival skills. He was old, tired easily, didn't understand traffic.

Catastrophic failure. He could not have screwed up more.

Sirens approached. Carter wiped his sleeve over his forehead to get rid of the damp.

With Ivana gone, all his plans were ruined. How could he face Katie now? Or Bree. They'd called him, asking for his help, and he'd made things exponentially worse. He'd travelled over a thousand miles only to fail one of his closest friends.

"I have to find her," he said.

"Dude, they'll get the dog."

"No, not him. Her."

Carter finally managed to fit his fingers into the button and unclip his safety belt. The siren got louder and then stopped, the ambulance parking behind him.

Carter stood. He swayed a moment, blood rushing to his head.

"Woah, buddy. You better sit back down," the young man said.

An older man with an accent said, "Yeah, you don't look so good."

Hands pushed Carter back into his seat. He gave no resistance. The best thing now would be for him to die. He'd never have to face Katie or Bree. He'd never have to hear of Ivana's fate after he failed her.

Two paramedics rolled up with a stretcher and began asking questions. The onlookers answered as best they could, and then a tall paramedic with curly hair leaned in and started taking Carter's vitals.

"Can you hear me, sir?"

Carter nodded.

"Are you having chest pains?"

He shook his head. "Not my heart."

A blood pressure cuff went around his arm.

"You felt dizzy? Light-headed? What?"

"I have a…a disease."

"What disease, sir?"

"I don't know."

He cursed his stubbornness. He'd never wanted to know what was killing him. Didn't want to give it the respect. They regarded him like the old fool he was, not even being able to name his disease, even if it helped him. Probably assumed dementia. An escapee from a nursing home somewhere.

"Do you have a doctor we can call?"

"In Minnesota."

"Minnesota, huh? Do you have a number?"

Carter shook his head again. All that was written down in his kitchen on a pad next to the refrigerator.

"Okay. We'll get you taken care of, sir."

They eased him out of the car and onto the stretcher. The second paramedic, a woman with a tight bun of brown hair and a gold cross around her neck, placed an oxygen mask over his mouth.

He wanted to tell them about Ivana. He'd sound crazy, he knew. He had nothing solid to tell them except it had been a white van. All he'd seen was her getting in. He could give no description of the two men who took her, didn't have the license plate, or the make and model of the van. He had a blurry image in his mind, a hearsay theory of who the men were, and no idea where they would have taken her.

Not exactly an airtight case against them. Not to mention an unregistered gun in his car.

The onlookers who'd helped him drifted away. Carter felt the stretcher crunch across the sandy ground of the median he'd stopped on, then reach the street and push into the air-conditioned confines of the ambulance.

The woman stayed in back with him, while the tall man went to get behind the wheel. They'd come alone, no police escort. Nobody to tell his story to. If he didn't die on the way, he'd have to find someone at the hospital to tell. He needed to do something, even after everything he'd done so far had crumbled and fallen apart, because he didn't know when to stay home.

He was out running around the country with nine toes in the grave.

The tall man radioed in with a lot of jargon Carter didn't follow. The female paramedic prepped an IV line and asked if he had any allergies that he knew of.

Carter shook his head.

The oxygen fed his lungs like he'd risen from the depths. The pain in his gut had subsided. In that way, the worst was over. For Ivana, the worst had only begun.

The needle slid into his arm expertly, and she held it in place with white tape.

"Ready to roll," she called. She stood, hunched over in the small space, and reached for the back doors to shut them in.

Carter heard a familiar sound. A single bark, then another.

He moved to sit up, rattling the IV line and bag hanging from a hook over his head. He said, "My dog," but the mask muffled his words.

One more bark reached him, a more desperate sound like pleading for help, and then the doors slammed shut.

She sat back in her seat, and as she went down, he tried sitting up.

"Woah there, sir. You need to lie back."

"My dog," he said again. She looked at him, swiveled her head the way Chester did sometimes.

"Your what?"

He pointed at the closed back doors. "Dog. Dog!"

Chester barked again, and the vehicle rocked as he put his front paws up on the back of the ambulance.

The siren started up and drowned out all other sound. The gurney shifted under Carter as the vehicle dropped into gear and began to roll forward.

He looked her in the eye. If his words didn't land, maybe the plea in his expression would. Carter reached out and took hold of her hand and squeezed harder than he thought he could right then.

"Hang on!" she shouted.

The ambulance came to a stop, the stretcher shifting and banging against the partition separating the front and back.

She leaned forward and opened one of the rear doors. Chester took two bounding steps and put his front legs into the rear of the ambulance. He sniffed the air, then, with some effort, pushed off on his back legs, and the rest of him tumbled inside. Less than elegant, but he was in.

"Hey, hey, no. I can't have a dog in here."

Chester was sniffing in overdrive, running his nose along Carter from foot to head in the stretcher. A low whimper came from his throat.

"Seriously. He can't stay."

"I can't leave him."

The siren cut off.

"What's up?"

The driver looked through the narrow gap between the front seats and the rear and knew immediately what the problem was.

Chester, satisfied that Carter was there and wasn't dead yet, turned his attention to the woman, telling him he couldn't stay. He sniffed, he licked, he whined.

"What do you wanna do?" the driver asked.

Chester pushed his muzzle under her hand, demanding attention and scratches.

"It's fine," she said. "Let's just get there." She leaned forward and shut the rear door. She said to Carter, "He can't come inside the hospital."

Carter nodded. "Thank you."

The siren kicked back on, and they began moving again.

"You're lucky I'm a dog lover."

Carter didn't consider himself lucky in the slightest right then.

"Have you ever considered getting some therapy?"

MJ spat out the open window. "What for?"

Luke couldn't quite believe he wasn't getting it. Then again, he was beginning to understand that MJ had no self-awareness at all.

"For, like, anger management or something. You stabbed that guy in the foot."

"He was giving me shit."

"Still, dude…"

They'd only managed the three illegals in the back of the van. That would fill out the first batch of ten, but then leave them with an uneven number, and since they didn't seem to be paying for anything under an even ten, they needed to get work. But not today. Not with an injured man in the back.

Luke wanted more help. Different help, anyway. MJ alone was turning too unpredictable. Maybe he could get two others to help out, send MJ with one, and he'd take a new partner, and they could round up twice as many that way. Sounded like a plan. Faster, more efficient, more money in the end.

"Let's drop these three, and then I want to call Marco. We should split up. Get twice as many that way."

"You mean, like, let me have my own crew?"

A crew of one, but let him think what he wanted. "Yeah. You need to get a van or some kind of car to keep them in."

"I can do that."

"Okay, good. I'll call Marco from back at the house."

Luke steered the van toward home.

"I was thinking," MJ said, his eyes on the view out his window, one arm propped up and fingers tapping a beat on the roof. "We should get more cash with that bank deal. We could pay guys a flat fee up front and not cut anyone in on the back end. Less to split, we can pay them less than a full share since they'd be getting it right away."

"More for us," Luke said.

"Yeah."

Luke was never a fan of taking unnecessary risks, but he was a huge fan of getting more of a percentage. The crazy thing was, the perfect people to help them would be the parking lot workers, who they could pay fifty bucks for the day. He toyed with the idea. Say he'd pay them, get them to help grab some others, then at the end of the day take them too. He wouldn't have to pay any of them that way.

He seriously doubted he could get any Mexicans to snatch their own kind off the streets, though. He needed patriots. True believers. White men intent on making America great again.

It would be funny, though, to work both sides of it that way.

* * *

Ivana tried to calm down the praying woman. She explained to her in Spanish about Carter. That help was on the way. As soon as they arrived, they'd be rescued.

She didn't seem to understand at first.

"*¿Cómo te llamas?*"

"*Patricia.*"

"*Patricia, todo estará bien.*"

Ivana took her zip-tied wrists, made a hoop of her arms, put them around Patricia and hugged her tight. The man on the floor hadn't let go of his foot, but at least he'd stopped whimpering. Thick swooshes of red criss-crossed the floor like an abstract painting.

The van slowed and then stopped. She listened as the front doors closed, footsteps came around to the side, and then the side door rolled open, blasting a white burst of sunlight into the darkened van.

"Let's go. You first."

Patricia was taken from the van, then the second man reached in for Ivana. She got out and immediately scanned the area for Carter's car. She waited for maybe gunshots, a warning shout, some surprise attack, but nothing came. She studied the yard, the surrounding homes in what she found was a normal, suburban street. She tried memorizing the surroundings in case she needed to describe them later, but none of the street names meant anything to her; the landmarks were useless.

The van door was slammed behind them, sealing the injured man inside, and the two women were hustled around the side of the house. Carter hadn't leapt in to save them yet.

Ivana figured he was waiting to get her inside so she wouldn't be in danger of crossfire. Maybe he had some larger plan for reinforcements, maybe the young man from the restaurant who clearly had a crush on Katie.

They were hurried to a smaller building at the end of the driveway. Multiple deadbolts and a steel security door were the only indication this was anything more than a simple detached garage.

The door slid open to reveal a sparse open space with two other women in it. Ivana and Patricia were shoved inside. The men shut the door behind them and left.

"Are one of you Isla?"

Isla brightened at her name, then a wash of concern came over her.

"Who are you?"

Ivana tried to explain succinctly. When she mentioned Marta, Isla cut in.

"Is she okay?"

"Yes. My daughter and her friend are taking care of her."

"Oh, thank God." Isla began crying. Deepti looped her arms around her.

"We have someone coming to help us. He will be here any minute."

"Help?" Deepti asked. "Who?"

"A friend. He's done this kind of thing before. Sort of. We made a plan."

"Is he police?"

"No."

"Then how is he going to help?"

The door opened again, and the two men each had the injured man held up by his armpits.

"Everyone, stay put," MJ said. To make sure nobody got any ideas, he went to his waistband to draw his knife. The injured man slid off MJ's shoulder.

Luke said, "Wait, wait. Hold it!"

It was too much. The injured man slipped from Luke's grasp. He let the man drop, side-stepping as he fell. The injured man collapsed, his head slapping the concrete floor with a hollow sound.

"God dammit," Luke said. "C'mon."

He grabbed MJ by the shirt and pulled him out of the garage, slamming the door behind them and leaving the injured man to the women.

Ivana waited for him to move, but expected him not to.

Deepti was the first to move toward him. She crouched and touched his shoulder.

"Sir?"

He groaned. All four women went into action. They laid him out flat, checked him for broken bones, made sure he was breathing.

"Is this the guy who's supposed to help us?" Deepti asked.

"No. He was in the van when they took us. He'll be here soon. He'll get us out."

She said it, but inside, she wondered what the hell Carter was waiting for.

So this is how it ends.

Carter listened to the steady beeping soundtrack of his imminent death. His arm was sore from the IV line, his back sore from lying in bed. The dull off-white walls of the hospital room, the bland LED lighting, the sand-colored linoleum floor easy to mop the blood from all combined to look like the saddest waiting room for heaven or hell he could imagine.

He'd recovered from his latest attack, mostly. His midsection was still sore, and his head throbbed, but that also could have been dehydration and lack of food. Also, the panic of losing Ivana and the weight of guilt crushing him from all sides.

The blinds were open, and his view was a parking lot and a dark brown stucco building next door. Not the California from the postcards. Not what he wanted his final view to be.

The door opened, and a young doctor entered.

"Mr. McCoy," he said, reading off the chart. "Glad you're up. I hate waking patients." He smiled in a practiced way, like he'd read a book on bedside manner. A nurse followed in behind him, and she went straight to the machines to check the readouts and add the numbers to Carter's chart.

"I'm Dr. Nguyen, nice to meet you. We've been in contact with your doctor back in Minnesota, and he filled us in on your history. He was also surprised to hear you were traveling."

"I bet he was surprised to hear I was still alive."

Dr. Nguyen smiled and let out a breathy chuckle. Carter knew he'd been spot on, but the young doctor was ashamed to admit he'd discussed Carter's unlikely survival with his colleague.

"How are you feeling now?"

"Hungry. Thirsty. Sore."

"Okay, we can deal with all three of those things."

"Do you have my phone? I need to call some people and let them know I'm here."

The doctor looked to the nurse, who opened the drawer on a small side table and brought out a plastic bag with a few of Carter's things in it. She fished out his cell phone and handed it to him. It might be easier to use his frail condition as an excuse to make them call Bree, but then he got his courage back and knew he had to be the one to tell them about his failed mission.

"Thanks. Do you happen to know where my dog is?"

"Your dog?"

"He was with me in the car."

The nurse set down his chart, her entries complete. "I think the paramedics still have him. Big dog? Brown and tan?"

"Yeah. They do?"

"Last I saw, but that was an hour ago or so."

"Mr. McCoy," Dr. Nguyen said, getting the conversation back to his agenda, "we want to be able to make you as comfortable as possible. As you know from your diagnosis, there isn't anything we can do long term—"

"I just want to get out of here."

"I think it's a good idea if we monitor you for a day or two."

"You talked to him. You know I'm gonna die. But you have to believe me, if I don't get out of here, other people are gonna die too."

Dr. Nguyen furrowed his brow. "I'm sorry?"

"It's too much to get into. I'd like to be released. That's all. I don't want to die in a hospital."

"I don't recommend that you drive—"

"I'll call for a ride. I don't know where they towed my car to, anyway."

"Mr. McCoy, I really recommend–"

"I'm checking out."

Carter scrolled his phone contacts and found Bree. He pressed CALL. Dr. Nguyen got the hint that the conversation was over. He handed the file to his nurse and turned to leave.

"Best of luck, Mr. McCoy."

Carter addressed the nurse, "Can you give me a minute?"

She followed the doctor out of the room and closed the door. Carter took a deep breath, and Bree answered.

"Oh my God, where have you been? How's it going?"

Katie came and sat on the arm of the couch, fingers worried into knots as she pulled and picked at her cuticles. She whispered, "Put it on speaker."

Bree did.

"Hey there," Carter said. "I have some news."

"Okay, what?"

Carter cleared his throat. Bree braced herself for bad news. It was worse than she imagined.

"I'm at the hospital."

"Oh my God, Mom," Katie said.

"No, no. Just me." Carter swallowed, his mouth dry. "The thing is, your mom's not here. She got into a van. I tried to follow but…"

Bree waited. Katie picked at her fingers.

"But what?"

"They got away."

The steady beeps of Carter's machinery sounded in the pause as Bree and Katie tried to understand what he was saying.

"They got away? What's that mean?"

"I started to follow, but I had an attack. I must have passed out. I woke up, and the car was on a median, and there were people all around and an ambulance."

"Holy shit."

"Yeah." It sounded like Carter might be crying. "Girls, I'm sorry. I'm so sorry."

"What are we gonna do?"

"Can you come get me? We'll figure something out. I can't do anything from in here, though. I don't know where the car is."

Katie leaned forward toward the phone. "My mom, is she…?"

"We'll find her, Katie. I promise. I swear."

Bree hated her choice to call Carter. She should've gone to the police and taken their chances. She should have done something herself. Instead, she relied again on this old man. This *dying* old man. How could she? And now this. Katie's mom in danger. Missing and maybe being shipped off to some detention center or some detainment camp. And after that, who knew?

They'd heard the horror stories, seen the photos. Both the ones with Democrat lawmakers trying for some sympathetic angle to get people to stand up and speak out, and the gleeful smiles-and-thumbs-up glamour shots of the administration proudly posing in front of cages built for humans. Both were horrific, but the proud ones made Bree sick to look at. Camps built in swamps, in deserts, lacking the most basic amenities. Places where people went and were never heard from again. Places where rights and respect were checked at the door. And Ivana was there now, or headed there soon.

But they weren't going to give up. If Carter wasn't the one who would save Ivana and Isla, they'd do it themselves. Somehow. Someway. She broke away from her old life, done the impossible once. Time to do it again.

"We're on our way," Bree said.

Luke reached through the narrow gap of the open door and underhanded the McDonald's bag. It landed with a wet thud on the concrete floor. He shut the door before anyone could react or make eye contact.

Inside the house, he sat down and opened the wrappers on two Big Macs of his own. He needed to get more whey protein powder, more creatine. He was getting soft. Since he'd stopped picking up part-time construction jobs to get scum off the streets full-time, he'd been sluggish and slow. He'd been expecting a call from his old foreman begging him to come back, but nothing had come. Last time he drove by the most recent site where he worked, the place buzzed with activity. Mostly brown skin. Two more floors had been added to the building, and a retaining wall for the landscaping that was to go in the front courtyard. Things were speeding along.

His phone rang, and he quickly licked special sauce off his fingers before answering.

"Hello?"

The voice was deep, breathy, and crunchy with gravel. "You ready to clean this world? To scrape it clean from the pests and the insects?"

"Who the hell is this?"

"You ready to cleanse it in fire?"

"Fuck off."

He hung up. Freaks. Some religious group? He had Jesus, and he didn't need anything else. God said it, he believed it, that settled it.

The phone rang again. He dropped his own voice low and mean this time. "Hello?"

"Shit, man, you can't take a joke?"

It was Marco, laughing at him.

"You say something funny, and maybe I'll laugh."

"Aw, lighten up, you prick. Listen, I got a hot tip. Better than a racehorse at Santa Anita."

Luke wiped his mouth with a thin napkin. MJ came into the living room and sat down, his burger and fries spread out on a plate like a dignified gentleman.

"Yeah?"

"A place over in West Colinas. Landscape supply warehouse. Nothing but illegals. Ten or fifteen to a shift. Like shooting fish in a barrel."

"You want us to just go in and scoop them all up?"

"Shit, yeah, man. Five grand a pop? Get out your biggest net and let's go fishing."

Luke looked at MJ, who was waiting eagerly to hear what the conversation was about. He thought about the numbers they needed to make up for the short load last time. The payments not yet received. His dwindling back account that left him eating fast food. Stupid little town didn't even have an In-N-Out.

"When?" Luke asked.

"First thing tomorrow morning. You bring yours and I'll bring mine and between us we should bag at least eight, maybe more."

"Okay. You swing by here, and we'll follow you."

"Not gonna thank me for the tip?"

"Once I got a full load, then I'll thank you. Until then, you can suck my dick."

"Son, that'd be all the thanks I need." Marco laughed, which was abruptly cut off when he ended the call.

MJ said, "Well?"

"Big score. First thing tomorrow."

"Hell yeah."

MJ took a bite of his burger and stuffed his mouth so full he could barely breathe.

"Is this all they feed you?"

Ivana looked at the limp and half-squished burger in her hand.

"Yeah, pretty much," Deepti said.

It had been too long, and Carter hadn't shown up. Something was wrong.

"So, where is this man?" Isla asked.

"I don't know. He should have been here by now."

"In other words," Deepti said around a mouthful of food, "he's not coming." She swallowed. "No one's coming."

"If he said he would help us, he will. Carter wouldn't leave me behind."

"Is he your boyfriend or something?"

Ivana shook her head. "Just a friend." She folded the wrapper around her burger and walked it over to where the injured man leaned against the wall, his eyes squeezed tightly shut.

"Here," she said. "You can have mine."

He opened his eyes, looked from her to the burger, then held out his bound hands. She placed the burger in them gently, as if it might break.

"*Gracias.*"

"*¿Cómo te llamas?*"

"Emiliano."

She looked at the crude job the women had done of wrapping his foot after trying to clean the wound as best they could.

"*¿Duele?* Does it hurt?"

"*Un poco.*"

"That's good. You eat."

"*Muchas gracias.*"

Ivana walked back to where the women sat with their backs to the cinderblock wall, eating the meager food.

"Do you know where we are?" she asked.

"No," Deepti said. "We drove less than an hour after they picked me up. Didn't feel like any highway driving, either. But I couldn't tell you where we are."

"I was so scared," Isla said. "I don't know how long we drove."

"There were others when we first arrived," Deepti explained. "They sent them away. I heard them say something about delivering them. I assume to some sort of ICE facility. That's what this all is. They're bounty hunters. Goddamn executive orders offered up money for any illegals. I don't think they really care about anyone's actual immigration status, though."

"How is that legal?" Ivana asked.

Deepti laughed.

"My sister," Isla said to Ivana, "was she scared?"

"No," Ivana lied. "She is strong."

"And my parents?"

"I didn't hear anything about them." Ivana looked around the basement. "So how do we get out of here?"

"Sister, we've been thinking about that for two days now," Deepti said. "If you figure it out, let us know."

"There must be a way."

"Our best chance is when they take us out of here."

"To bring us to ICE?"

"Yeah. But they have guns. One man has been shot already." Deepti's eyes moved to the spot where Juan had fallen and the dark stain of blood that remained.

Ivana followed her gaze, recognized the stain, and shivered as a rush of cold moved through her. "Really?"

"Yeah. An older man. He was trying to protect his wife."

Deepti left it there. She didn't explain what happened to the man's body.

"It won't be us," Ivana said. "Either Carter will come to save us, or we'll do it on our own."

Normally, Bree would have seen the parking rates and said "Screw that", and gone to find street parking, even if it had been a mile away. Today was different. She pocketed the parking ticket from the hospital visitor lot and crossed over the drive leading to the Emergency Room entrance.

Katie followed close behind her. She hadn't said much of anything since she learned that her mother was missing. Her concern for Carter had been dwarfed by a near panic about her mother. Ivana was exactly the kind of person who was no longer safe in America. A good citizen, hard working and contributing to her community, but only a citizen through marriage. Someone no longer married. Widowed, technically.

She fell into the category of the vulnerable under the new watchful eye of white men intent on reforming the nation in their image.

They'd left Marta with a neighbor, Mrs. Borgeson, a widow who loved looking after Marta any chance she got. She promised to fill her with too many cookies and chocolate milk.

As Bree reached the door, a mournful howl caused her shoulders to lift, her eyes to squeeze shut. She hated hospitals for just such a reason. The suffering that went on, sometimes in the name of healing and sometimes in the act of dying. Whatever pain compelled someone to cry out like that made Bree tense up and nearly cry out herself. The sound called again, and she recognized a familiarity to it. It couldn't be Carter. He'd never complain that loudly.

But it could be Chester.

Bree turned and saw the dog straining at his leash. A woman, no more than five foot two, held on with two hands in a losing battle against Chester's recognition of someone he knew.

"Katie, look."

They veered away from the hospital doors and crossed to a courtyard where the woman, dressed in a navy blue shirt and pants combo with paramedic patches on the sleeves, a gold cross hanging around her neck, struggled to keep Chester in hand.

"It's okay," Bree said. "We know him."

Bree bent down and let Chester come sniff her. It quickly turned to sloppy kisses and excited chuffing.

"Do you know the owner too?" the paramedic asked.

"Yes. Carter McCoy."

"Oh, thank God. Here." She relinquished the leash, and Bree took it, though Chester wasn't going anywhere.

"How did you get Chester?" Katie asked.

"I picked up the old man. He's lucky it was the end of my shift. And this one is lucky I'm a dog person. If it had been a cat…no way." She reached down and scratched Chester on the head. "We've been hanging out, but I need to get home."

"Thank you so much," Bree said.

"No problem. Is he doing okay?"

"Carter? Yeah. We're here to take him home."

"Oh, good. Good luck with this one. He's been mostly sleeping, but when he sees a squirrel or something, look out."

"Yeah, that's him."

The paramedic waved and walked away.

"I'll stay here with him," Katie said. "You go get Carter."

Bree handed over the leash and went inside.

* * *

Carter had nothing to do but sit and try to think of a plan. It had been hours and he had exactly nothing. The pain meds didn't help his focus, but he had

131

nowhere to begin his search for Ivana.

When the door opened, and Bree entered, tears welled in his eyes. He expected her to come at him yelling, accusing him of losing Ivana forever. Her fate resting squarely in his hands, and he'd let her slip through. Instead, she came in with her own wet eyes and took slow, quiet steps toward him.

"Hey, how are you?" she asked.

"Still here. Somehow. I'm sorry."

"What happened?"

He explained about seeing Ivana get into the van, starting to follow, and then blacking out, coming with people all around, Chester gone, and an ambulance siren wailing in his ear.

"Chester's downstairs with Katie right now."

"Really?" He let out a breath he'd been holding for a long time. "And you can get me out of here?"

"Nobody said we couldn't. So let's go. We have to get them back. No time to waste."

Carter sat up, tore the tape from his arm, and slid the IV needle out of his vein. "I think my clothes are over there."

Bree got him a plastic bag with his pants and a shirt. His shoes were at the foot of the bed.

"I'm sorry I let you down," he said.

"You didn't. Not your fault."

"I don't know what made me think I could do this."

"You helped me when nobody expected it."

"That feels like forever ago."

"It wasn't. And now you have me and Katie with you. We're not letting them take her, or Isla. Or anyone else."

Bree handed Carter his shoes, then she turned around so he could take off his hospital gown and get dressed.

Carter and Bree stood in line at the impound lot right as it opened at eight a.m. He paid the fine and got the rental car back. The first thing he did was check the center console, lifted the stack of napkins, and found the gun. Nobody had found it, as he feared they might.

They'd discussed the night before what the new plan would be. Nobody had a great one. The phrase "needle in a haystack" had been said more than once.

It was decided that something was better than nothing, and that they would make the rounds of other spots where people frequently lined up for day labor work, or where rumors had it that people had been taken before.

Bree invited Orlando to come along, and he brought his cousin, ChiChi. ChiChi's car was a mid-60s Imperial repainted in gold flake with tiny tires, pinstripes across the hood, and a gold-plated display in the back window that said MIDNIGHT RAMBLERS AUTO CLUB.

ChiChi was about twenty-five and thick in the middle. He smiled a lot, laughed even more, and Carter thought he may have been high. His real name was Indigo, but nobody called him that. Carter welcomed ChiChi to the search crew.

Between them, they had three cars. Carter, with Chester riding shotgun, Bree and Katie, Orlando, and ChiChi.

"I say we split up," Carter said. "Cover more ground."

Bree nodded. "If anyone sees anything, call, and we'll come join you. Don't let them get away."

Carter winced at the slight dig, but knew Bree didn't mean anything by it.

They stood in a circle, and Katie walked them through downloading an app where they could track each other's movements.

"My mom put this on my phone ever since I was, like, six." She'd immediately gone to the app when she learned Ivana had been taken, but there was no signal. Her phone had to be off or destroyed.

Bree input an address into Carter's phone as a place for him to start.

They all agreed to keep in close contact, and then all drove off in opposite directions.

* * *

"You scared the crap out of me, you know," Carter said. Chester gave him a look back that said, *same, old man*. Carter scratched the dog behind his ears. Chester had dealt with the change in scenery well, but Carter assumed he wanted to be back at home napping on the couch as much as Carter did.

He followed the GPS voice across town to a parking lot in front of a home improvement store. He immediately clocked three guys huddled in the corner, shuffling their feet as if they'd already been standing all day. They'd probably gotten there before seven, so it had already been several hours. By now, work was unlikely to show up. The desperation for a job made them easier targets for the fake ICE agents.

He parked and decided to watch for a while.

* * *

Inside the car, things were tense with Katie. Bree understood why. If her own mother had gone missing, she might not care much, but she knew how much Ivana meant to Katie, and vice versa.

Bree tried to reassure her friend. "We'll get her back."

"I hope she doesn't try to do something stupid. She's not really the sit around and wait type."

"Yeah, I know. But that's a good thing."

"What the fuck's going on with this country?"

"I honestly don't know."

They drove in silence until they reached an industrial laundry facility. Trucks loaded with linens from hotels and motels across the city rolled in and out, dropping off and picking up. Plumes of steam rose from pipes on the roof. Men pushed around bins filled with dirty sheets, towels, restaurant uniforms.

Bree parked across the street. Nobody looked scared. Nobody hung in dark corners waiting or watching them, except Bree and Katie. Business as usual.

"What should we do?" asked Bree.

"I guess wait here a while? I don't know."

"Might as well." Bree turned up the radio.

* * *

ChiChi never stopped his car. It prowled like a shark, a low rumble from the V-8.

"So, who are these friends of yours, man? Taking on ICE? That's badass, son."

"The old dude just showed up. They knew him from where they lived before. They don't talk about it back then."

They turned a slow left at a stop sign. "Well, it's cool, man. I've been wanting to take it to these fuckers for a while now."

"Scary shit, man."

"Yeah, no doubt."

They cruised slowly, each man looking out their side of the car for anything suspicious. "My cousin's friend got taken. Sent him to El Salvador, man. That dude was born in Oaxaca."

"Yeah, it's messed up."

ChiChi took another left. "So what's with you and Katie, dude?"

Orlando blushed. "I don't know. Nothing, man."

"You gotta make something happen. She's fine."

One of his biggest fears was that someone else would swoop in while he hemmed and hawed, working up the courage to make his move. But she knew he liked her. She had to. Anyone could see his lovesick routine around her. Customers asked her out daily, and Orlando had to stand and watch. If he could rescue her mom? He'd be in.

"I will," Orlando said. "It's gotta be the right time." Like right after a tearful reunion of mother and daughter.

"Shit, if you're not gonna hit that, I will."

"No." He turned his attention away from the street to focus on his cousin. "Don't you dare."

ChiChi smiled. "Chill out, bro. I'm just sayin', it ain't gonna be there forever, y'know?"

"Yeah, I know. I know."

ChiChi pointed out the front windshield. "Hey, what's that?"

A sand-colored van was pulled to the curb a half block ahead of them. It looked as if it used to be owned by some business, but the old logo had been either poorly scrubbed off or poorly painted over, leaving the ghost of some old writing on the side.

Two women were talking to whoever was inside. They each held bags in their hands, like maybe cleaning supplies for a day job as a maid or in some office.

"Check it, check it," ChiChi said.

Orlando sat up straight, leaning forward in his seat as the women turned their heads as if they were taking notes about their surroundings, a little nervously. They acted tense, jittery and ready to run like squirrels stealing from a bird feeder. After a moment, they nodded to each other as if agreeing to something and then got into the van.

"What was that?"

"That's pay dirt, man, is what that is. We got 'em."

"Holy shit."

ChiChi gunned the engine, but Orlando put out an arm across his chest. "No, no, man. Don't spook 'em. Just tail them, let me call the others."

"Yeah, right. Cool."

ChiChi dropped the Impala back down into shark mode and fell in behind its prey as the van pulled away from the curb.

* * *

Carter's phone rang. He picked it up.

"We're in business," Orlando said. "I'm dropping you a pin."

"A pin? How do I use a pin?"

Orlando grunted a frustrated sound. "Just use the app, man. But catch up to us. We got them."

The line went dead. Carter opened the app that Katie had set up for him, and he could see a small circle with Orlando's photo in it moving about a mile south of him. Much further away was a circle with Bree's face. That circle was already moving toward Orlando.

Carter put the rental in gear and turned toward the circle.

Luke hadn't cleaned out the back of the van so there were still smears of blood making two crude Xs across the floor. He and MJ followed behind Marco and a friend of his, Dean, who he'd brought along. Dean only stood five foot seven and Luke thought Marco liked having him along because he made Marco look even bigger than he was. His take on Marco from the day he met him was a man who wanted to intimidate, to be seen as the Alpha in every situation.

Luke wanted to earn respect through his brains and good ideas, not brawn. Though brawn helped.

Marco extended an arm out the window and pointed to the left, directing Luke where to turn. Then Marco's van turned right. They flanked the landscape supply warehouse on the East and West side streets.

They parked and got out.

Before they left the house, Luke had swapped MJ's pistol and knife for a taser. MJ argued it for a minute, but then warmed to the idea of jolting fifty thousand volts through someone. For Luke, it was self-preservation. He didn't want to have to bury another body. At least with electricity, MJ couldn't spill any more blood.

"Zip ties?" Luke asked.

MJ patted his back pocket, and Luke could see the plastic stems poking out like a bouquet of dead flowers.

They met up with Marco and Dean on the sidewalk. Both men wore desert camo outfits head to toe. Steel-toed boots. Luke had on his tactical vest that looked bulletproof, but was in fact a fishing vest he got at a Walmart. His store-bought badge hung around his neck.

"Okay," Marco said. "You can carry, what, six? Seven?"

"Eight at least if we cram them in."

"Eight's gonna be hard to manage."

Luke pictured the money, the bodies still to get paid from the last run. "We got it."

"Okay then. Goin' in hot."

Marco pulled a gaiter up over the lower half of his face. Stitched to the jacket over his biceps were a patch of the American flag and another of the Department of Homeland Security he bought off eBay.

Marco drew a Glock from a hip holster and gave a primal scream, then charged toward the front door. MJ hollered, the sound muffled from the full-face balaclava, and followed close on his heels. Dean went next, and Luke brought up the rear, both their faces covered as well.

When they entered, announced by Marco's primal scream and drill sergeant shouts to shut up, line up, get on the ground, the response was immediate.

Several workers called out, "*Immigración. Immigración.*"

Bodies scattered. Two men pushed past Luke and body checked him like hockey players. Men dropped whatever they were carrying and ran.

The four men yelled for everyone to stand still, but nobody listened. MJ eagerly fired his taser and caught a man in his calf with the long string of wire and the metal spike at the end. The man went down and grunted, clutching at his leg, but then pulled the prong out and got up again in seconds.

Gathering one at this rate would be difficult, but eight was going to be impossible.

The first dirt clod hit Luke from behind. He turned, thinking it was a fist and he'd have to grapple with someone. About fifteen feet away were three men, all with torn-open bags of planting soil at their feet. They were grabbing fistfuls of dirt and throwing it at the men.

Once the others caught on to this new tactic, a barrage of projectiles rained down. Clay flower pots, wood chips, mulch, bags of bird seed. Then came the rocks. River stones, landscaping rocks, handfuls of gravel.

The inside of the warehouse became a cloud of flying debris.

They hadn't captured a single person among the four of them, and they were getting pummeled.

A rock hit Luke behind his ear, and he spun, gun out and searching for the culprit. A warm line of blood moved down the back of his neck. Dirt and wood chips came from every direction.

"Ah, what the fuck?" Marco shouted. He fired a single round straight up, hoping that would scare the men into submission, but it had no effect. A large plaster garden gnome crashed at his feet, and he stumbled backward.

"Let's get out of here," Luke said.

"Fuck that," MJ said, and he fired his taser again. It missed its target, and before the wires could retract, he took a scattering of gravel across the face. He shouted and stumbled backward, trying to claw tiny rocks from his eyes, the only part of his face that was exposed.

Dean was doubled over trying to wipe a manure-based soil mixture out of his eyes, nose, and mouth. He gagged and looked like he might throw up.

"Fall back!" Marco said.

Luke grabbed MJ by the collar of his shirt and pulled toward the door. The shouting of the workers got louder when they saw the men start to retreat. A mixture of Spanish and English, Luke heard "Fuck ICE," and "Get out of here, pig," clearly.

Little bombs of succulent plants in clay pots began raining down on them from somewhere deep in the warehouse. They appeared out of nowhere from behind a tall set of shelves like little grenades, exploding all around the retreat and spreading soil and greenery across the concrete floor.

"Go, go, go," Marco said, sounding like he was deep in a PTSD flashback of traumatic combat experience.

Luke backed out first, pulling MJ with him. Before the door shut, a worker emerged from the rows of shelving holding a metal rake in front of him like a spear. He poked Dean in the chest, rattling his ribcage with a straight shot to his sternum, and knocking him on his back. A cheer rose up from the workers.

Luke stumbled back and pulled MJ down on top of him. They fell in a pile on the walkway to the front door, the taser falling away to the side. A moment later, Marco burst out the door, still holding his gun. His camouflage outfit now stained with dirt and mud.

Luke got to his feet, and MJ got to his knees, scanning the ground around him for his fallen taser gun.

"Leave it," Luke said.

"No way."

From the roof, a twenty-five-pound bag of cow manure crashed to the ground and exploded, sending a dark brown cloud of aromatic dirt for twenty feet in every direction. Luke looked up to see two men with another bag held between them, swinging it back and forth for momentum.

"Leave it," he said again. This time, MJ listened.

The second bag of manure landed a foot behind MJ as he ran, splattering their backs in retreat.

Dean tumbled out the door, did a full somersault through the manure, then got up and ran.

When Luke turned the corner, he found six men crowded around his van. In unison, the men shouted, "One, two, three", then Luke watched helplessly as the van leaned up onto two tires before it came crashing back down with a crunch of metal and screech of shocks. He took off in a sprint, wishing he had the taser. He could fire into the air, but that came with consequences. He knew his badge wasn't real, and if he fired a shot, he'd have to answer for it, executive order or not. Chances were good he'd get off even if he killed someone, but it could take a year and a costly court case before he could expect to be pardoned.

Again, the six men chanted, "One, two, three!", and the van tipped. Luke got there just as the van rolled onto its side. The men cheered as glass broke, metal scraped the pavement, and the air filled with the tangy smell of fluids leaking from the underside of the van.

MJ leaped onto the back of one of the men. He tried to take him down, but only ended up going for a ride. The other five men all jumped in and pulled MJ off, tossing him aside like he weighed nothing. They began chanting "Fuck ICE. Fuck ICE. Fuck ICE."

Luke saw one of the men pull a lighter from his pocket. "Let's go!" Luke shouted.

MJ scrambled to his feet and fell in behind Luke. When they reached the corner, Luke looked back as a small flash of yellow billowed up into an orange and black cloud as his van erupted in flames.

It was hard to miss ChiChi's car. Carter zeroed in on it ahead and was grateful he didn't have to keep looking down to check the app anymore. He'd nearly sideswiped two other cars and a mailbox on his way to catch up to Orlando and his cousin. Now that he had them in sight, he tapped on the most recent call in his phone, and Orlando picked up.

"That you back there?"

"Yes. Where is it?"

"Ahead of us, like a block and a half. You said hang back."

Carter tried to see, but couldn't make out which vehicle they were following.

"Maybe I should take the lead spot. That car you're in isn't exactly subtle."

There was a pause. "Maybe you're right, man."

Carter accelerated. "What color is it?"

"Like, off-white. Kinda. I dunno, tan maybe?"

Different than what Carter saw Ivana get into, but maybe his attack had blurred his memory. Then again, he'd never be able to forget seeing her taken away and knowing it was his fault.

He eased past the Impala, and Orlando nodded as he drove by. He hadn't heard from Bree or Katie yet, but they had farther to go to catch up.

He spotted the van, the faded writing on the side, and fell in behind it with four cars in between them. The van drove conservatively. Kept to the speed limit, stopped fully at stop signs. They rolled quietly another five miles across town until it pulled into a strip mall parking lot.

Carter noticed quite a bit of California was covered in these one-story outdoor strip malls. And endless supply of nail salons, check cashing businesses, cell phone stores, and liquor stores, one of which the van pulled in front of.

Carter parked, and the Impala eased in next to him. Bree and Katie had caught up and parked a few spots down. The driver of the van got out and went inside the liquor store. All a normal day in the suburbs.

Orlando came to Carter's window.

"What do you think, man?"

"I don't know. You think they have people inside?"

"We saw two women get in."

"Forced in or they got in?"

"Seemed like they got in, but they looked nervous."

Carter studied the van, then the front of the liquor store. "Why'd they stop here?"

Chester barked once, and Carter turned toward the sound. ChiChi appeared at the passenger window. He held a gun.

"Yo, what are we waiting for?"

"Hey," Carter said. "Put that away."

"I thought we were gonna take these guys down."

Carter got out. He moved as quick as he could. "I said, put it away. 'We' aren't doing a damn thing. I am. And we're not doing it out in public."

"Shit, man, then why are we even here?"

"To get people back. And not just the people in the van right now. People they took before. That's not the way to do it."

Carter hadn't noticed the driver come back out until Orlando tapped him on the shoulder.

"Uh, dude…"

Carter looked up. The van driver stood by his open door, a plastic bag in his hand with whatever he'd bought inside. He was looking across the lot at them, eyes wide at the gun in ChiChi's hand.

"Shit," Carter said.

The van driver made a quick scramble into his vehicle. ChiChi gave a hoot and took off across the lot. Carter moved back around to his car door.

The van squealed tires as it pulled away. ChiChi ran after it, the gun waving out ahead of him. Bree got out of her car and said, "What's happening?"

All Carter knew was that he wasn't going to lose that van again. Beyond that, he had no plan. Stealth was gone, so he charged across the lot and fell in behind the van as it hit the street. Behind him, the big V-8 of the Impala roared to life as Orlando started it up, leaving ChiChi behind. Fine by Carter. He didn't need a wild card in the mix.

The cautious van driver from before was gone. The van swerved and cut off other drivers. He barely slowed when he reached a four-way stop sign intersection. Carter had to let him go and watch as a half-block gap developed between them. But no way was he going to let them get away.

He didn't worry about the potential damage to the rental car as he gave chase. Nor did he think about traffic laws or police. If they got stopped, then he would explain about the van and hope that the police would help him track down Ivana. It certainly wasn't any sort of official government agency vehicle he was chasing. These abductions were of the vigilante variety, he was sure now.

The grumble of the Impala's engine rattled Carter's windows as Orlando pulled alongside him. Carter didn't take his eyes off the van for a second to acknowledge him.

Orlando surged ahead.

"Don't do anything stupid, kid," he said, even though only Chester could hear.

Carter opened the center console on the rental. The gun sat there, ready to be called into action. Easier now to reach than being an arm's length away in the glove box.

The Impala came even with the van. The impeccable paint job, the custom fixtures, all at risk if he tried to bump the van off the road. ChiChi would never—but Orlando…?

The van took a hard right, and Orlando had to fight to turn the Impala in time to follow. Carter hung back, satisfied now to be in second position.

Chances were slim they would be leading them to wherever they had Ivana and Isla kept. Maybe they were fool enough, but he doubted it. The best bet now was to stop them and force them at gunpoint to take them to save the women. Cater also knew these men were likely armed as well. He'd deal with that when they came to it.

Orlando caught up with the van again, a new reckless vigor in his driving. He pulled even, then ahead. Bits of gravel kicked up and pinged off the windshield of Carter's car. Brake lights flashed red on the van as the Impala cut a sharp right in front and cut him off. Smoke came off the tires as the van skidded and rocked on its shocks. Carter braked. He waited for the sound of an impact, the van colliding with the Impala.

The van stopped cleanly, only inches away from ChiChi's custom paint job.

An SUV and a sedan passed Carter, speeding away from the mayhem. Carter put it in park, reached for the gun, and got out. Chester barked behind him, either a warning or encouragement.

Carter made a wide arc and held the gun at the ready down by his hip. He faced the driver's window. The man behind the wheel held his hands out in plain sight. He was breathing hard, fear and panic on his face.

Carte raised the gun. "Keep those hands up."

In his past helping other people, he had taken more of a shoot first, ask questions later approach. He couldn't kill this man. He needed to know where Ivana was.

"Get out of the van. Get out!"

The driver complied. Carter could hear him speaking in Spanish. That didn't make a whole lot of sense.

The side door slid open, and two women were there. Each on their late 30s, each looking terrified.

Orlando ran in from the front of the van. He was amped up, ready for a fight. He grabbed the driver and tackled him to the ground.

Carter looked at the women and said, "You're okay now. You're okay."

Orlando wrestled with the driver, each exchanging loud Spanish. Carter hung back, ready for trouble, listening for police sirens.

Orlando stood up quickly. "What?"

The driver spewed rapid-fire Spanish, his voice cracking. He pleaded, gestured to the two women.

"What's he saying?" Carter asked.

"Hold up, hold up."

The man kept talking. He held his hands together as if in prayer, begging Orlando for understanding.

"Shit, man."

"What?" Carter asked.

"It's not them." Orlando backed away three steps, letting the adrenaline flush away. "This is his brother's wife," he waved a hand toward the women. "They're helping her get away from an abusive marriage."

"What? What are you saying?"

"We got the wrong guy. This guy is just helping someone leave her husband. They assumed we were sent by the brother."

"*El detective,*" the driver said.

"He thought you were some kind of private eye or some shit."

Carter lowered his gun. "What?"

"He saw ChiChi and the gun, and he thought…I dunno man. It's not them." Orlando turned to the man and offered a hand to help him up off the ground. "*Lo siento.*"

Carter quickly put the gun in his waistband. "We gotta go," he told Orlando. He apologized to the women as he rushed back to his car. Orlando got the message and hurried back to the Impala, shouting a few vague explanations and apologies in Spanish over his shoulder.

Carter pulled away first, and then the Impala burst to life behind them. They sped away, leaving three very confused citizens.

Carter took several deep breaths. His hands were shaking on the wheel. He wasn't even paying attention to where he was driving; he just had to get away.

The close call, the near tragedy if ChiChi had gotten out of hand or if he himself had not gotten the whole story, combined with the crushing realization that they were no closer to getting Ivana back, made him pull over.

He put the rental car in park and shut his eyes. Chester leaned over the back seat and sniffed at Carter. He lifted a hand and scratched Chester's head.

The phone rang.

"Hello?"

"You okay, man?" Orlando had pulled to a stop behind him, the Impala in idle.

"Yeah. Just need a minute here."

"Fuck, man, that was…messed up."

"Can you call Bree and Katie and tell them we're fine. Tell them false alarm."

"Yeah, man. You sure you're okay?"

"Yes. I just need to breathe."

The isolated cell was getting to Ivana. The space shrank around her, the air getting thinner.

"This is crazy," she said.

"Beyond crazy," Deepti said. "It's kidnapping. It's harassment. It's a huge fucking lawsuit once we get out of here."

"*If* we get out," Isla said.

Ivana could see the defeat on her face. The worry had turned to hopelessness. Ivana wasn't there yet.

The injured man groaned and rolled over where he was trying to sleep in the corner. His foot had swollen badly, the skin red and warm to the touch. Infection had set in. He needed medical attention.

"We should make them get him to a doctor," Ivana said.

Deepti ran a hand through her short hair. "There's no making those assholes do anything."

"He's going to lose that foot. Or worse."

"Then he'll have a hell of a lawsuit, too."

A door slammed outside. The boys were back. Muffled shouting came through the walls, but it didn't sound like they were coming to the garage. Ivana listened, but couldn't make out anything.

* * *

"What the fuck am I gonna do now?" Luke said. "That was my van, dude."

MJ went to the fridge and got a beer. He didn't bring one for Luke. "What

149

the hell happened?"

"They were, like, organized."

"That was freaky."

Marco had circled around and picked them up after they'd run five blocks to get away from the angry mob. As they drove away, Luke could see the column of black smoke from his burning van.

Everyone traded conspiracy theories on the drive back, how they knew they were coming. Who snitched. Who paid for professionals to be there? Nobody considered that they'd attacked a place where people were sick and tired of being harassed.

The worst part, they'd come away empty-handed. No new deliveries and now no van.

"What are we gonna do?" MJ asked between sips of beer.

"Get more money, first of all. Then get me another van."

"How are we gonna do that if we can't turn in the ones we have?"

"We go back to the bank. Or a different bank, but we do that again."

MJ nodded. "Yeah, yeah. We get a bigger score this time. Enough to buy a new van."

"Exactly."

MJ had a realization. "Aw, shit. I lost my taser."

"We'll get another one. If we only take what we did on the last bank, we'll need to hit a few. We gotta blitz it. Bang, bang, bang before they can spread the word and get ready." Money for a new van would be great, but starting over money would be better. Dump this whole business and get a fresh beginning in a new place. Maybe find a compound in Idaho or somewhere with like-minded patriots.

Luke stalked the living room, checking out windows for people watching. He knew they had to have been tipped off. Somebody must have spilled. Marco? The new guy, Dean? But he got the worst of the violence, so maybe not him. Something went colossally wrong, though.

Luke checked the time on his phone.

"I don't wanna wait. If we hit them right at the end of the day, they'll have more cash on hand." He didn't even know if that was true, but it sounded good.

"Yeah, you're right. But how are we gonna do it without the van?"

"We'll take your car. We only need two of them. We take the girl who did it right last time; she can follow instructions. And then maybe the new one. Leave the one with the attitude."

"Where can I get a new taser?"

Luke thought about it for a second. "Fuck it, take your gun. We need to do this right."

"Hell, yeah." When MJ smiled had tiny flecks of dirt and manure still in his teeth.

They gathered at the restaurant, Bree and Katie both chipping in to wait on the three customers inside. Carter sat at the short counter under the surfboard mounted on the wall. They'd set a bowl of chips and salsa in front of him, but he ignored it. He stared into his water cup and worried about how far from a solution they were.

Orlando had been dropped off by ChiChi, who tore away in a cloud of burnt rubber smoke. The Impala could have been much worse off than the few paint chips missing from the spewing gravel kicked up during the chase, but ChiChi was mostly mad that Orlando had taken the car when it was understood ChiChi was the only one to drive his baby. Now, Orlando paced behind the counter, full of nervous energy and hoping that Katie didn't think less of him that he'd led them on a fruitless chase and still not found her mother.

They'd tied Chester out back and put down a plate of meat and rice for him.

A man came in and ordered a burrito and a drink to go.

Bree sat next to Carter.

"It could have gone a lot worse."

"All I know is I've let you down," Carter said.

"No, don't say that."

"You called me when one person was missing. Now there's two, and one of them is Katie's mom and probably my best friend in the world. That's not exactly solving your problem for you."

"Shit happens."

"Yeah."

The feeling reminded Carter of the same helplessness from when his daughter died. The world, suddenly out of his grasp, spinning like a carousel, broke loose. No matter how much he wanted to do something, to make things right again, a solution pulled away forever out of his grasp. The last time he felt this way, it was twenty years before he could do something about it. He didn't want that to happen again.

Orlando handed the man his burrito. He wore a tank top with hairy shoulders poking out, board shorts, and flip flops. The mandatory uniform of this little coastal town, as far as Carter could tell.

The man opened the bag to check its contents and frowned.

"The fuck is this?"

He took out the burrito and set it on the counter.

"I said carnitas."

"Is that not…?" Orlando looked closer. It was a fish burrito. "Aw, shit, sorry, man. My bad."

"Why don't you fucking pay attention? Do your job."

Carter kept his hands folded in front of him, his face turned toward the man. "Hey, cool it." *Did people say cool it anymore?*

"Mind your fuckin' business." He balled a fist, slammed it into the burrito, making a flat mess on the counter. "I'm not eating this shit."

"Yeah," Orlando said. "We'll make you another one."

"Not *another* one. Carnitas this time, dipshit."

"Sorry, that's what I meant."

"And I'm not paying for it."

Carter thought about the gun. Thought about all the things he'd done in the past year. The unexpected looks on the faces of the men he'd stared down before pulling a trigger.

"Not today, mister."

Carter stood, the tank top man ignoring him, and turned to the surfboard. He lifted it from the bracket, mounting it to the wall like a stuffed marlin. Turning a full hundred and eighty degrees, he smashed the board into Tank Top's back. The man pitched forward and flopped into the counter. Carter dropped the board, grabbed the man by the back of his neck, and shoved his face into the countertop.

"You're not being very nice," he said. "You're trying to act tough, but if I had to guess, you don't really know what being tough really is."

"Let go of me."

"Okay."

Carter let go and backed up two steps. Tank Top spun, looking for who had attacked him. That same look of surprise hit his face when he found a man in his seventies with anger in his eyes and not a hint of fear.

"Fuck this place, man." Tank Top swept his arm across the counter, knocking over a plate, which went smashing to the floor.

Finally, Carter could do something. His pent-up rage and undirected frustration found their target.

"Still not nice," he said. Carter bent down and picked up a shard of the broken plate. He held it in his hand and stepped toward the man. "Now somebody has to clean that up."

Carter stepped hard on Tank Top's left foot. That diverted his attention long enough for Carter to move close to him, put the shard of plate to his neck, and made him feel the pressure. Tank Top stopped all movement. Carter could smell the sunscreen on him.

"Now, should it be you that cleans that up?"

Tank Top quickened his breath. He spoke, quiet and slow. "He fucked up my order."

"And you think that gives you the license to be an asshole?" Carter pressed the broken plate harder against his throat.

"No, no, it doesn't."

Bree spoke in a calming voice from behind him. "It's okay, Carter. Let him go."

Carter knew it wasn't about this customer. He stood in for all the men Carter couldn't find. The men who'd taken Ivana and the girl, Isla. Men who thought they were above any punishment. Men who posed and preened. Men who wore tank tops.

"Okay," Carter said. "Everyone makes mistakes, right?"

"Yeah," Tank Top said. "Yeah, everyone."

"I could make a mistake and slide this sharp edge over your carotid artery. That'd be a big mistake, huh?"

"Please. I'll apologize. I'll clean it up."

"Carter," Bree said, a little more forceful this time. "Let him go."

Carter eased back the pressure on Tank Top's neck. "See? I respect these people, so I'll listen."

He stepped back, still holding the shard, but out of arm's reach in case Tank Top wanted to start swinging.

The man looked to Bree for some sort of assurance, then around to Orlando, and finally back to Carter. He ran through the open door and kept running.

Carter dropped the shard of plate.

"I'll get a broom."

* * *

Carter sat on the back step, petting Chester. There was an odd kind of comfort in the gas the old dog emitted after his plate of spiced pork and chicken. It made Carter feel at home.

Bree came to sit next to him.

"You okay?"

"Not really, no."

"You feel like you might have another episode?"

Carter set his elbows on his knees and folded his hands in front of him. "It's not a health thing. I came here to do a thing, and I blew it. So far, it's just a big goddamn failure. Well, that makes me feel bad, and I'm tired of it."

"Is that why you blew up at that guy?"

"That guy was an asshole."

"Yeah, true."

Chester lay down at Carter's feet. "If I don't make it," Carter said, "y'know, before this is done...you're gonna be all right, won't you?"

"What does that mean, don't make it?"

"You know what it means."

Bree set a hand on his. "Carter, if you're not up for it, I totally get it. It was a lot to ask. Too much. I don't want to put you at risk."

Risk is all he had to offer, though. His job was avenging angel. A cleansing rain. Men who treated the world like it owed them more, who treated people like they were subservient, they deserved what they got from him because they were bound to never get it anywhere else.

But he was tired. He kept making things worse. They'd be better off without him, maybe.

He'd been thinking it a lot lately. Go out on his own terms. The brief stay in the hospital worried him. It was the last place he wanted to spend his final moments. Now, he had a gun. Someone to take care of Chester.

Yes, he'd be leaving things undone, but wouldn't that be true no matter when or where he went?

He wanted to do more. Needed to do more, but if he failed again, it would crush him down smaller than he already was. The end of the road had come.

"You, stay." Luke pointed a finger at Deepti, but she kept her eyes on the gun in his other hand. "You two, move."

Ivana looked at Isla. Isla hung her head and walked toward the door.

"Where are we going?" Ivana asked.

"Out. Move," Luke said.

"Out where?"

Hands shoved her from behind. MJ pushed her toward the driveway beyond the door. "Just get going."

They weren't taking everyone, she noted. Why were they separating her and Isla? The injured man, she could understand, but why leave Deepti?

"That man needs a doctor," she said.

"He'll be out of here soon," Luke said.

Three steps down the driveway, Luke stopped. "Shit."

MJ put a hand on Ivana's elbow. He tensed, on high alert. "What?"

"My wallet. I didn't put it in my pocket because I usually do my keys at the same time, and now that I don't have a goddamn van—" He huffed out a breath, frustrated all over again over his lost van. Luke aimed a finger at Isla. "Stay close."

Ivana got to see the inside of the house for the first time since she was brought in as they passed through it, Luke gathering his wallet and sunglasses from the kitchen counter. This was a mistake they'd made, and she wanted to take advantage of it. She tried to remember as many details as she could. The color of the walls, the number of rooms, anything that might help identify this place. She still didn't even know their names.

Luke tucked his gun away. "When we go outside, no talking, no shouting. You walk straight to the car, and nothing happens. You get cute, things get ugly."

He didn't wait for a response. MJ opened the door and walked out, taking his keys out of his pocket as he walked down the path. He scanned side to side for prying eyes. Luke and the women stayed behind, watching the street and waiting for MJ to get to the car.

"Where are you taking us?" she asked again.

Luke got right in her face. "Are you fucking serious? Just go outside and get in the car and stop asking stupid questions."

Ivana backed up until she hit a small console table in the entryway. Isla put her zip-tied hands on Ivana's arm. "Just do what they say."

"Listen to your friend here," Luke said, and he shoved Ivana's shoulders. Her hip banged into the console, and she sucked in air at the sharp pain. She turned and grabbed her hip.

"It's okay," Isla said to Luke. "I got it." She leaned in close to Ivana. "I think I know where we're going. We did it once before. It'll be okay."

Ivana nodded, her eyes pointing down. On the table was a small pile of mail. The top envelope was a letter offering a pre-approved credit card. One that had Luke's full name and address on it. She put her hands over the top and closed her fingers around it.

"Okay," she said. "I'll go."

As she turned back around, she folded the letter in between her hands and pressed herself into Isla's back. Using her as cover, she pushed the folded letter into her front pocket. Outside, MJ's car was idling at the curb in front of the house. Isla led, Ivana followed, and Luke came last, closing the door behind him.

During the drive, they explained the plan. Isla had heard it before. Enter the bank, pass a note to the clerk. Take the money. Leave without saying a word.

"I'll be watching you," Luke threatened.

"We'll be fine," Isla said.

"Let's hope your friend feels the same way."

Ivana ignored him, doing her best to clock every street sign she saw as they drove out of the neighborhood and toward the first bank.

Carter and Chester were alone out back of the taco shop. The smells were familiar ever since Ivana had schooled the cooks in her special techniques. The music was more modern than at Mesa Grande, but it put him in mind of better times.

He was glad he'd stopped by to see Audrey and Ava before he left. A last goodbye.

He'd grown his whole life thinking of California as a place of opportunity, of reinvention. West had always been the direction of infinite possibility. Now he knew the hard truth of it. If you came West and things didn't work out, there was nowhere else to go.

The end of the line.

Maybe some people looked out over the vast ocean and dreamt of sailing away, or hopping a freighter and starting over on the high seas. But most people reached the sand, and that's where it ended for them. No more running, no more chasing. The West Coast was a place where all roads came to an end.

Carter felt the weight of the gun in his pocket. He'd held that weight before, and it filled him with memories of the men he went after. Men who'd done him or people close to him wrong. Now the weight had become his burden to carry. He kept adding to it, stone by stone, until he could no longer bear the load, and it dragged him toward the water, holding him under the waves beyond where the sunlight can reach. He found it harder to resist the pull.

Chester grumbled and shifted at his feet. He lay on his side and let out a long breath, never once opening his eyes. He was ready to say goodbye to it all, everything except the old hound.

Carter decided to stay there with him a little longer, carrying the weight until it finally would break him at last.

Luke kept his head down, baseball cap pulled low. Cameras everywhere these days.

He'd explained to Ivana until she knew her instructions. Walk to the teller on the right. Isla would approach the window on the left. Both women would hand over notes, both would take whatever cash they were given, and walk out quietly and calmly. It shouldn't look like a bank robbery. But he made it clear that he was there, armed and ready, if things didn't go according to plan.

He hated MJ's car. A four-door Honda in a dull brown color. Cloth seats with mysterious stains. A rip in the fabric on the ceiling. A/C that barely worked. He needed another van, or a large SUV. He'd always wanted a Hummer.

They walked in with ten minutes to go on the bank's posted hours.

This bank didn't have marble floors or vaulted ceilings. There was navy blue carpet that would look at home in an airport. Desks with fake wood veneer, plastic plants in the corners. Piped in music that sounded vaguely familiar, but not quite right, like a memory of a story misheard.

One loan officer sat at her desk near the back wall, typing at her computer. No other customers were inside. Most bank tellers must be pretty bored these days with everything happening online and barely anyone using cash anymore.

Could be why of the six teller windows, only two had women behind them.

Isla and Ivana stepped forward at the same time and handed over their notes.

* * *

Ivana waited for her teller to read the note. A name tag read: DENISE.

Denise looked at her with a half smile, but it dropped away when she read the fear on Ivana's face.

"You want me to…"

Ivana whispered, "Cell phone."

"What?" Denise checked the note again.

Ivana couldn't raise her voice. She tried leaning closer. "Cell phone."

Denise sucked in a quick breath. "Oh, no, I won't…"

Ivana shook her head very slightly, trying not to alert Luke. "Get out your cell phone. Make a call."

"A call?"

Ivana huffed. "Get the money. Start to get it."

Denise opened her drawer. She glanced over to her fellow teller and could tell she was in the midst of the same actions. Two robbers, both women.

"Get your phone out," Ivana said. "Keep it low."

Denise didn't understand, but she followed orders.

"Dial this number," Ivana said, and then read off Katie's phone number. "Keep the volume low. Don't let him hear." She shifted her eyes to where Luke stood at the narrow counter for filling out deposit slips. She turned back and locked eyes with Denise. "Tell her it's her mother."

"What is this?"

"My last chance."

* * *

MJ waited outside.

If Luke could get a new van out of this deal, maybe he could get a new car, too. His run-down Honda was a bigger shitbox than that van ever was. And why should Luke be the only one to benefit? He was going to have to use the money they got from the bounties to pay for a new car. Luke got to use this bank money. Hardly seemed fair.

He was glad to get his gun back. Made him feel like a wild west outlaw. He'd have done well back then. A man on his own, taking what was his. Manifest destiny and all that. The real American dream. Get all you can, and may only the fittest survive.

Nobody he knew was more American than MJ. He understood how the whole system worked.

He checked his watch. Closing time. They'd have the place all to themselves. Maybe a perfect chance to make a bigger score than just some cash drawer at a teller window.

He ducked inside before the guard could lock the door.

* * *

God dammit, what was he doing inside?

MJ stood next to Luke, hands in the pockets of his jacket. Luke knew that meant one hand on the grip of his gun.

"You're supposed to be outside."

"Doors are locked," MJ said. "Nobody else is coming in. So it got me thinking."

"You don't have to think. You just had to wait outside."

Luke checked the progress of the women at the counter. He followed the guard with his eyes as the man made his way to the side door by the ATM vestibule.

"We got all the time in the world now," MJ said. "What's in that vault?"

* * *

Denise thumbed down the volume until there was only one bar. She kept the phone on the counter in front of her, hidden from anyone else's view.

Another quick look to Luke, and now MJ stood with him. Probably not a good sign, but a perfect distraction for her. She caught Denise's eye and

164

raised her eyebrows, trying to let her know this was the moment.

Katie answered. Ivana tensed and motioned for Denise to talk.

"Tell her."

Denise bent at the waist so she could speak quietly but loud enough to still be heard, all while still pulling cash from her drawer. "Is this Katie?"

"Yes. Who's this?"

"I'm here with your mother."

Carter bent down and kissed Chester on the top of his head.

"Best choice I made in the past ten years," he told the old dog. "Hope I made it okay for you. Bye, buddy."

He walked away and out into the parking lot. Chester stood watching, his leash keeping him tied to the railing of the back steps of Surfside Tacos. He licked his lips, hopeful that Carter would be bringing back more food.

He'd been to Florida with Ava, and every afternoon they were there, it rained. Only for about ten minutes, but a downpour that would flood the sidewalks and parking lots and leave the air a humid mess. Here in California, every afternoon, they got a lovely breeze that came in off the ocean and cooled the air, even the heat coming up off the asphalt. Around him, men walked in shorts with thick sweaters over them, ready for both the heat of the day and the cool chill of the evening.

Nobody here had ever seen anything like a Minnesota winter, and they didn't seem to miss it a bit. Yes, maybe it made them soft in some ways. But what good was being hardened by your environment? What did it accomplish for Carter?

Wasn't being content and happy better in the long run?

He hoped his choice wouldn't make Bree angry or too sad. They all knew it was coming, so nobody had a right to be too upset. But this way was best. He wouldn't have to see another morning where he'd let everyone down.

He wouldn't have to see Katie's face as she worried where her mother was.

* * *

"Carter!"

Bree rushed out the back door, but only found Chester, jolted awake by her excited approach. She turned a one-eighty, but didn't see him. Katie was inside, still on the strange phone call. Ivana had found a way to reach out. They knew where she was.

"Carter?"

She went back inside and knocked on the restroom door. "Carter?" She tried the handle, it was unlocked and empty inside.

The restaurant wasn't big. Nobody could be inside without them knowing. He had to be out back, still. But where?

"Let's hurry up, please!"

Luke grabbed MJ and pulled him close. "We're sticking to the goddamn plan." Luke tried to keep his voice down, but it was hard if MJ was going to keep pissing him off like this. Plans meant nothing to him. Always going off on some wild idea that just popped into his head.

"But it's all sitting right there," MJ urged.

"God damn." Luke faced the teller windows again. "Can we hurry it up there?"

Ivana said to Denise, "You have to hang up. Don't let them know you have the phone."

She'd only had time for Denise to let Katie know the address of the bank and that her mother was there, but not what her mother was currently doing. Katie had taken some convincing, which wasted more time. Ivana couldn't raise her voice loud enough for Katie to hear, and she couldn't bend down close enough to the phone to whisper because of the bullet proof barrier between them. And if Luke was getting impatient, she had to trust Denise would do the rest.

Isla took the bag full of cash from her teller. She hadn't spoken a word, whispered or otherwise.

Ivana spoke softly. "When they come, send them here." She placed her palm down flat on the counter. Denise kept looking at her like she was missing something in this interaction. She was robbing the bank, but she also seemed to want help. The girl on the phone was crying now, but Denise hung up without saying goodbye.

Ivana took her hand away and left behind the letter she'd taken from the house. Denise understood and placed a flat hand over the top and slid it into her now-empty cash drawer.

"Let's go!" Luke said.

Denise passed the bag of bills to Ivana.

"No police," she said. "When he comes, send him." She mouthed *thank you* and turned away, hoping Denise would come through.

* * *

"Is there a problem, sir?"

Luke jumped at the new voice. The security guard had snuck up on them.

"No, no, we're fine. Just…women, y'know?"

He tried a smile, but it came across forced. The guard wasn't convinced.

MJ didn't wait. He drew his gun and pushed it in the guard's face, almost touching the skin under his right eye. The guard was older, late fifties probably, but still fit. All these guys were ex-military or ex-cops. You could tell by the high and tight haircut. He should sign up for ICE, MJ thought. Better gig than this one. Fresh air, cleaning the streets, good pay.

"Mind your fuckin' business."

The guard, calm as can be, lifted his hands. "Due respect, sir. This is my business."

"You know what the fuck I mean."

Isla and Ivana joined them. "We have it," Isla said. "We can go."

Luke grabbed the back of MJ's shirt. "Come on. We're done here."

MJ kept the gun raised, and the guard studied his face as they backed out of the bank. Ivana caught the eye of Denise and pleaded with her. She saw a hint of understanding there, a willingness to help behind the confusion.

Outside, MJ pocketed his gun. Luke let his full rage fly.

"Get in the fuckin' car. I'm sick of this shit, man. Now he's seen us. They got cameras. Jesus Christ."

He took the bags from Isla and Ivana, then shut the door on them.

* * *

The other teller came over to Denise. "You okay?"

"That was the strangest thing."

"I know. I'm shaking, my God."

The guard bent over a desk and punched the button for an outside line. "I'll call it in."

"No, wait. Don't," Denise said.

The guard waited, the phone halfway to his ear. "What? Why?"

Denise recalled the interaction, the fear on the woman's face. She snuck a glance at the envelope in her drawer, then closed it so the other teller couldn't see. "Nothing. Never mind."

The guard resumed his call.

"I know how you feel," the other teller said. "That was crazy."

Denise said, "I need some air." She turned and picked up her purse, waiting for the other teller to do the same. When she did, Denise opened her drawer and slipped the envelope into her bag. She went outside to wait for the police. She would give her statement and tell the truth. Most of it.

He walked toward the breeze. It made him think of the sand. If he'd come all this way, he might as well do it at the beach. The place where the road ran out.

Carter turned around and walked toward his car.

Bree came bursting out the front of the restaurant.

"Carter! We found them. She called!"

Like a wave after its crashed to shore, all the feelings flowed out of him. The negativity, the fear, the self-loathing.

Bree reached his car. "We know where they are."

He reached in his pocket and touched the gun. A new feeling now.

"Tell me."

FOUR

He made it clear—only him. Carter wasn't going to endanger Bree or Katie, and he didn't want a wild card like Orlando or any of his relatives. Everything else he'd done on his own, and this he needed to do as a solo. What he didn't tell them is that he had to make up for his failures. He needed to show himself that he could finish this.

"You call us as soon as you know anything," Bree said.

"I will."

"I think we should be close, at least," Katie said. They'd looked up the address of the bank the teller had called from. The teller couldn't answer all Katie's questions, and the call had been cut short anyway, but they knew Ivana had wanted Carter to come there. The bank was across town, about nine miles away.

"Okay," Carter said. "You follow and then find a place to stop and wait. Take Chester with you."

He'd lost him once and wasn't going to let that happen again.

"Hey, wait, hold on," Orlando said. He jogged back inside the restaurant.

Carter stood close to Katie and put a hand on her shoulder. "I'll get her back."

"I know you will."

"Your mom was smart to do that. I want to know what they were doing in a bank, but I guess we'll ask her when she comes home."

Orlando came running back. He held a sawed-off shotgun.

"What the hell is that?" Bree asked.

"We had it in back. Todd, the old manager, put it there. Y'know, just in case."

"That thing even work?" Carter asked.

"I don't know. But here's some shells." He handed the gun and the dented box of shells to Carter, who put them in his front seat.

"Thanks. Might come in handy, but I hope not."

"You sure you don't want help?"

Carter shook his head. "I work better alone, I think."

He climbed in his car and set the GPS. He paused for a second. It wasn't the dramatic exit he wanted, but he climbed back out of the car, and to respond to everyone's curious looks, he said, "Gotta hit the men's room first."

With age had come the indignities of the weaker bladder. But once he got on the road, he didn't know when he'd be able to stop again, and better to get it out of the way now than to get the urge at an inopportune time.

He went in and unzipped his pants. He let out a long breath, trying to calm his nerves along with relieving himself. When he looked down, he said to himself, *well, that's new.*

The bowl was tinged with red. A good amount of red, actually. More than a tinge. That was blood, and that was a first. He stared at it for a long while until the water settled and the red swirled together to make a dark orange. He didn't know what to do about it. It wasn't a good time to rush to the doctor. He didn't feel any pain associated with it. All he could do was flush and file it away as something to watch out for next time.

He walked back out to the car, trying to dismiss his worry, and drove off.

"I want them out." Luke paced the floor, his heavy footfalls thudding like distant artillery. "Get them out, and fucking pay me."

MJ had a smile on his face as he counted the two bank bags on the kitchen counter. He ignored Luke's angry phone call.

Marco tried to calm Luke from the other end of the phone. "Jesus, take a pill. What's going on?"

"I just want them gone. We've had them too long. It's all…all fucked up."

"How many do you have?"

"Four."

"That's it?"

Luke kicked the coffee table. "It's enough. Add that to what we already delivered, and it's a full load, plus. Sixty grand. Supposed to be anyway. Are they still paying or what?"

"The government's been a little slow."

"A *little?* I'm starting to think this whole thing is bullshit."

"Hey, don't say that."

Luke pulled aside the curtain on the front window, checked the street, then let the curtain fall back into place. "Why not, huh? They keep making promises, and I haven't seen a whole lot of action, y'know?"

"Look, I'll come get them. I got a full load, and I can make the run. When I'm down there, I'll ask about payment."

"Why don't I just go with you? I can ask them myself."

"Nah, better if I go. Plus, I got my own guys with me. Y'know, security and managing all those bodies."

"See, this doesn't pass my smell test."

Marco stopped pacifying Luke. "Sack up, man. It needs to. These guys, the real deal Feds, they don't fuck around. These are the Alligator Alcatraz guys, okay? These are the fuck you, get on a plane to El Salvador guys. They don't give a fuck. You wanna get paid, go apply for ICE. Six-figure salary and five-figure signing bonus? Shit, why wouldn't you?"

Luke rubbed his temple. Yeah, and following orders, six a.m. call times, libtard democrat citizens shouting at you and throwing bottles. "When this is done, I'll look into it. For now, I want these people out of my house."

"I'll load up. Get 'em ready."

Luke hung up. He joined MJ at the counter. MJ smoothed the edges on six piles of bills, neatly laid out.

"Twenty-seven thousand, four hundred," MJ said. "Not bad."

Luke had to admire the stacks of cash. Of course, all of it would immediately go to paying for a replacement van, so it wasn't too much to get excited about.

"Marco's on his way. Let's get them ready to roll out. This isn't a fucking hotel."

Ivana questioned whether she should tell the others about what she'd done. She couldn't be sure if Denise would follow through, and she didn't want to give them false hope. She wasn't allowing herself much hope, but just hearing Katie's voice was enough to keep her optimistic.

Deepti wanted to hear all about it.

"Pretty much the same as last time," Isla said. "Walk in, give them a note, they hand over the money."

"It's like some Patty Hearst shit."

"Some who?"

Deepti rolled her eyes. "Before your time. Mine too, but I heard about it. Saw some documentary once. She got kidnapped by some political terrorist group, and they made her do stick-ups with a machine gun. When she got arrested for it, it turned out she'd fallen in with the group and become a member. Or something like that."

"That's what I'm worried about. They're gonna see that we robbed a bank, and no matter what, I'll go to jail for it."

"Girl, if we're around to get arrested and not in some detention camp in the Everglades, then I consider it a win."

Ivana stood over the injured man. The smell coming off his foot was foul. He spent most of his time sleeping, or trying to. Sweat glazed his face and his arms. He was burning with fever from the infection. If she had to guess, he was likely to lose his foot, maybe the whole leg.

"I tried something," she said.

"What?" Deepti asked.

"I don't know if it worked."

"What was it?"

She explained about the envelope, about passing it to the teller. About calling her daughter.

"She gave her the address?"

"To the bank. When they get there, she will hand over the envelope."

Deepti tried to process. "So, they don't know we're here."

"She will tell them."

"And this is the same guy who was supposed to be here days ago? The same guy who allegedly followed you here?"

Ivana nodded sheepishly. "Yes."

"Oh, great. That's great. Nice plan." Deepti slapped her hands against her thighs. "Why didn't you give it to the security guard at least?"

Isla stepped in to Ivana's defense. "It would have been impossible. She had a reason to be in front of the teller. I think it was a great plan."

"If it works."

The unanswered question hung in the stale air like another foul odor added to the funk of the holding cell.

Lights from three parked police cars flashed in the parking lot. The door to the bank was propped open, and the loan officer walked out, escorted by a suit-jacketed detective. Carter parked the car.

Katie had told him what she learned from the bank teller in their brief conversation: that Ivana was there, but not why. That she wanted to let Katie know where she was and that she was safe for now, but not why Ivana didn't make the call herself. The call ended abruptly.

Carter checked the scene for signs of violence. No ambulance, no coroner, no bodies under sheets. All good signs.

He got out and walked closer. Nothing had been taped off, so he could safely look around like a curious citizen drawn by the police activity. There didn't seem to be a sense of real urgency, which meant it wasn't a hostage situation or similar bank-related tragedy. He had no idea what Ivana would have been doing there and started to feel the whole thing had been a prank. But who would know Ivana was missing, and who would want to prank Katie like that?

He spotted two women sitting side by side on a curb. They were dressed in navy blue business attire and sipped from paper coffee cups. The kind the cops would give them while they told them to wait. One of the women talked quickly with animated hands while the other listened silently. The listener, with dark hair and a worried look, caught his eye.

Focused on the two women, Carter didn't notice the uniformed policeman who approached him.

"I'm sorry, sir, the bank is closed right now."

Carter startled. "Did something happen?"

"I'm afraid I have to ask you to move along."

"Yes, sir. I understand."

Carter walked toward where the two women were seated. The woman listening looked up at him again, holding his gaze. He didn't know what he was looking for, but each of them seemed to be waiting for someone.

He took a wide arc and reached the end of the parking lot, holding her eyes with his. He got to the sidewalk and stopped. She said something to her partner and stood. Carter put his hands in his pockets and waited.

With furtive glances back over her shoulder, she made it to where he stood.

"Are you the one who called?" he said.

She nodded, a look of relief crossing over her face. "Yes. I didn't know if it was real."

"Ivana was here?"

"I didn't get her name. What is this about?"

"She's in trouble."

Denise nodded again, her assumptions confirmed. "I thought so. I didn't tell the police anything about the call."

"Why are they here?" Carter asked.

"They robbed the bank."

Carter crinkled his brow. "Who did?"

"The woman. And another one. And there were two men with them."

He was missing enough of the story for it to make any sense, but he believed her. She reached into her pocket and withdrew a folded piece of paper, checked that nobody was looking, then handed it to Carter.

"She said to give you this."

He unfolded the letter, read a name and address. Ivana had been smart. He knew his next stop.

"Thank you."

"Can you explain all this?"

"Not yet. But you might have just saved someone's life. A few people, actually."

Denise became clearly excited about being a part of something secret and mysterious. Being robbed had not been the most thrilling part of her day, it turned out.

"So she'll be okay?"

"She will now," he said. "Thank you."

Carter turned and walked down the sidewalk, turning right back toward where he parked. Denise went back to her curb and her weak coffee.

Driving to kill a man. He'd been there before.

Carter wasn't sure what awaited him this time, though. In the past, he'd known exactly what his intentions were and who his target was. This time, his primary concern was in rescuing Ivana and Isla. Whoever fell in the crossfire, that would be their own fault.

The computer voice gave him directions. Just turns on a map. A maze leading him to the prize at the center. The self-loathing had gone, magically dissipated like fog over the ocean. He had renewed intent. He could rescue not only the missing women, but his own sense of purpose. Carter McCoy had been through his final act, done his curtain call, and returned for an encore. He had nowhere else to go when this was over, an empty list of things left undone. It could all end here, and if he returned Ivana to her daughter, it would be a life well lived.

Memories of all the men he'd gone after before rode with him in the car, but they didn't haunt him. They weren't chains around his neck. They reminded him of what befalls those who treat others with anything less than basic humanity. Show no respect, and you deserve no respect. Strip someone of their dignity, their basic human rights, and you show that you have none yourself.

Carter McCoy is here to make sure they understood.

"Your destination is ahead on the left," his phone told him politely. He tapped END ROUTE and pulled to the curb.

It had been proven to him before that evil could reside in such an average place. On a street where kids learned to ride bikes. Where block parties gathered on the 4th of July. Where somebody put a down payment on a house to live their American dream, now there were men stripping that dream away from others out of a misguided sense of grievance toward people that someone else told them were their enemy.

Did simple fools deserve to die? Maybe not. But when that foolishness devolves into cruelty and punishment of others, then they give up those rights.

Carter watched. He waited. The house didn't seem to have any excess security. He could see no cameras under the eaves, no high fences or guard dogs. Hiding in plain sight.

He knew there had to be some place where they were kept. The house was a single story, and there could be an attic under the pitched roof, but it wouldn't offer much space. This was California, so basements were a rare commodity. Maybe this was the home of the man who'd taken Ivana, but the captives were sequestered at another location. A strange space, an abandoned home, an old bomb shelter. He sensed they were close to finding them, but the realization crept in that he could still be as far away as ever.

Carter noticed the driveway that ran along the side of the house and disappeared into the back yard. No garage to be seen from the street. It wasn't a leap to assume a detached garage, out of sight and separate from the house, would be a good place to hold people against their will.

He got out, adjusting the pistol in his pocket. He left behind the shotgun. This was reconnaissance, not attack. Walking around with a shotgun in his hand wouldn't be very stealthy. He'd learned a while back that an old man didn't get much scrutiny on the street. He could use that to his advantage, but packing a sawed-off might tip even the laziest neighbor.

He passed by the driveway and turned to look. He was right that it led to a detached garage unit, two cars wide. He couldn't tell much about it from the outside, and walking down the driveway onto the property likely meant no going back. Telling, also, was the sedan parked outside the garage. So, no room inside for a car. Maybe the owner had a woodshop, maybe he had more cars inside, project cars in mid-repair. Or maybe he had Ivana and Isla in there.

He circled and passed again, getting a better look this time. The car meant somebody was home, but he'd been searching for a van. He made his way back to his rental and sat down to think. Circumstantial evidence at best, which hadn't worked out for the people he'd chased with Orlando. The vehicle he'd been after was nowhere in sight. Still…Ivana's gambit with the envelope meant more than the tiny details that seemed to be missing. He tapped a finger against the steering wheel. A cat crossed the street, paused to watch a bird land and then take off again, then moved on. Waiting. Carter had grown tired of waiting. He knew finally what he was going to. He had to make his move. Carter opened the back door and reached for the shotgun.

A truck turned the corner. A white cube truck, large enough to carry a significant cargo, but built on a pickup truck chassis, so easy to drive. A standard U-Haul he'd seen a hundred times before, but this one was unmarked and unremarkable.

Carter slid all the way into his rental and kept tabs on the truck from the front seat, the shotgun hidden from view.

The truck parked in front of the house, and a large man got out of the driver's seat, dressed in desert camouflage. Two men got out the other side, one in an untucked police officer's shirt with the badge still on his chest, and the other in all black. Not really a team, but clearly together. The cop's informal mode of dress told Carter he was off-duty. Maybe working this bounty scheme for some extra side cash. Still an officer, but not here in an official capacity. The others dressed like a screenwriter's version of an extraction team. Weekend warriors. The type who like to think they're part of the militia the framers talked about in the Second Amendment.

The large man marched straight to the front door with the cop trailing behind him. The man in black stayed behind near the truck. Carter kept his attention on the house. The two men were let inside. With the man in black all alone, Carter considered making a move on him. Possibly taking him out, but he still didn't know for sure if Ivana was inside or not. He needed all the information before he resorted to violence. Go off too soon and kill an innocent man, it meant he was no better than the men he hunted.

After five minutes with no other traffic on the street, the front door opened, and four men exited, each holding the arm of someone in zip-tie handcuffs. Ivana was second out the door.

Carter sat up straight. He could use a men's room again, but he pushed away the urge. Just nerves. The excitement of the moment. This was it, that moment of action. He'd never been so outnumbered. Never been so out of his element.

The large man pushed along a young Latina girl Carter assumed was Isla. He spotted a gun in the hand of a man behind Ivana who had ahold of another woman with short hair and dark skin who did not want to be leaving with them, that much was clear. She tugged and thrashed like a fish on a line.

The cop brought up the rear, helping along a man who limped and barely put any pressure on one foot.

The man in black walked with military precision to the back of the cube truck and flipped the lock on the back gate. With a shove, it rolled up, and Carter could see at least a half dozen men and women inside, all bound with zip-ties, all brown-skinned and scared.

Before thinking too long about it, Carter got out of the car. The lack of a solid plan took a backseat to his firm promise to not lose Ivana again. He left behind the shotgun. He needed at least a few steps looking innocent.

The large man clocked him first, but relaxed a little when he realized it was only an old man.

"Hey, any of you guys see a little white dog? Answers to the name Bella?"

Carter could feel recognition flash over Ivana. Her body tensed, spine straightened. He resisted the urge to make eye contact with her.

"Busy, pal," the large man said.

"Okay. Then how about, you see this?"

Carter drew his gun and pointed it at the head of the man holding Ivana.

Luke suddenly found a gun aimed at his head. How the hell had that gotten there? And who was this old man holding it?

The procession to the truck stopped.

"What the fuck is this?" Marco said.

"That's largely up to you," the old man said. "You let them go, and we all walk away. You want to make this go another way, at least one of you gets a bullet."

"Is this a fucking joke?"

"Come on, Marco," Luke said. The first bullet would go to him, so he wanted to do whatever he could to de-escalate.

"You are interfering in a government prisoner transfer."

"I doubt that. This isn't a government facility. I don't see any ID markings. You got something to show me? A warrant?"

MJ shoved forward, dragging Deepti with him and tightening his grip on her arm as she twisted to pull away. He thrust his gun at Carter. "We don't gotta show you shit."

The old man looked Luke right in the eye. "Tell him to drop it."

"MJ..."

"Fuck that," MJ said.

"Come on, god dammit," Luke said, a tremble in his voice.

"I can take him out," MJ said.

Marco kept a tight grip on Isla, with his other hand slightly raised in a show of good faith. "You're making a mistake, old man."

"Just let them go, and we can all move on."

Internal debates moved through the men. Nobody wanted to sacrifice Luke, least of all Luke, but MJ, Marco, and the cop all swelled with the confidence they could put down this elderly man before he did much harm. Before he got off a single shot, though? Doubtful.

While they were all thinking, the injured man made up his mind on how this would go. Summoning whatever small reserve of strength he had left, he swung an elbow backward into the face of the cop who held him. With a grunt and a splash of blood, the cop's head snapped back.

MJ jerked around at the sound of the commotion and fired. He'd been amped up, ready to shoot in time to stop Carter's bullet going the six inches into Luke's head.

The effort of the twist and pull of his elbow, and when the cop released him from his grip, sent the injured man crumbling to the ground like he'd been unplugged. By the time MJ turned and fired his wild shot, the injured man was on his way down, and the bullet caught the cop in his throat.

A blur of motion began.

Carter jumped at the shot, then turned his gun toward MJ. Everyone moved like a power switch had suddenly been flipped. The cop fell backward, a hand going to his throat which already spurted blood in a heavy spray. The man he'd held had fallen to the ground, groaning and reaching for his foot. The woman MJ had ahold of twisted away from him and fell to her hands and knees.

Marco reached down to his hip and drew a pistol from a camo holster that did its job, and Carter hadn't seen.

"Yo, yo, yo," Marco said, trying to control the situation.

While the gun still hung loose in Marco's hand, Carter spun on the big man and fired. Marco jerked back, his hand letting go of Isla.

Luke let go of Ivana and put his hands over his head as he crouched and ran toward the truck. Ivana ran at Carter, then veered off and dropped to scoop up Deepti.

The man in black left his post at the rear of the truck and went to Marco. Bodies spilled out of the open roll door at the rear of the truck. Men and women falling and tumbling to the ground, unable to break their fall with their hands zip-tied behind their backs.

The man in black got Marco to sit up, then turned and noticed the escape in progress.

"Go," Marco said. He brushed at the spot where Carter's bullet had flattened out against his Kevlar vest. He sucked in a few breaths, trying to fill his lungs again. Isla made a lunge for freedom, but Marco reached out a hand and grabbed her ankle, freezing her in place.

The man in black reached the back of the truck again and warned the others still inside to stay put, then grabbed hold of a woman who had tumbled out and held her down.

The cop arched his back, trying to cry out in pain, but his torn voice box wouldn't let him. He went still, and one more splash of blood pumped out between his fingers, then nothing.

Carter took Ivana by the hand and pulled her along, followed by Deepti on her left side in a chain of firmly gripped palms.

"My car," he said, pointing the way.

Two more shots rang out—MJ firing wildly again. Both shots went high and punched holes in the side of the cube truck. The man in black was forcing a woman back into the cargo hold and ducked his head and called out, "God dammit!" Two escaped men were up and sprinting away down the street in a stumbling run, unable to swing their arms.

Carter took aim at MJ, but before he could level a decent shot, the injured man on the ground swept his leg and tripped MJ. He clipped him across both shins, and with a yelp, MJ went down.

Marco had his breath back well enough to fire a shot at Carter. Whatever gun he had was big and loud, and it dug a divot out of the lawn by Carter's right foot the size of a basketball.

Carter needed to move. He returned fire toward Marco and hit the sidewalk, the bullet skittering up and off the door of the truck. He ran, knowing he was leaving behind the girl in Marco's grip. But he knew he couldn't help if he was dead.

MJ got to one knee and fired a shot nearly point-blank into the injured man. He instantly went from injured to dead as MJ's kill count ticked up by one more.

Behind him, Carter heard a bang, and he braced for a shot, but it had only been the man in black slamming shut the roll-up gate at the back of the truck.

He reached the car to find Deepti already behind the steering wheel.

"Get in," she shouted.

Ivana was in back. Carter opened the passenger door, reached in for the shotgun, and brought it around. The widespread of buckshot meant he had to watch where he aimed, and his eyes filled with the girl he figured for Isla. No matter what, he didn't want to hit her by accident. He tilted the barrel up and fired a single shot into the air over the group of men. They all ducked. Luke dove under the truck for cover.

Carter took two steps forward, eyes on Isla. Marco aimed and fired another shot from his canon of a gun. Carter ducked and flailed his hands, nearly dropping the shotgun.

"Carter!" Ivana called out.

He took another step forward, hoping for some separation between Isla and her captor. Marco tugged at Isla, pulling her toward the open front door of the truck and keeping her between himself and the advancing old man. Marco swung his arm over one shoulder and fired again, the bullet chipping the curb in front of the rental car's front tire. Carter knew he wouldn't be that lucky again. Isla was tugged closer to the truck, spreading the gap between them and lowering the likelihood of Carter reaching her with every inch she pulled away.

He knew to go after her then, and there was a suicide mission. Behind him, Deepti honked the horn.

MJ fired again, two angles of wild shots coming Carter's way. He backpedaled until he reached the rental car, opened the door, and took refuge inside.

Deepti dropped the car in gear and pulled away from the curb. Carter fumbled for his phone and as they passed, he snapped an off-kilter shot of the rear end of the truck, including the license plate.

Ivana could see Isla as they passed, her arm reaching out, eyes begging to be saved. The scream for help followed them down the street.

"We have to go back for her," Ivana said.

"Was that Isla?" Carter asked.

"Yes."

"Okay, let me drop you off."

Deepti took a corner too fast, and the back end fishtailed out. Carter told her to slow down; they were away from the danger now.

"We can't leave her behind."

"I won't," Carter said. "I need to get you out of danger. Bree and Katie are close by."

Carter handed his phone to Ivana, who called Katie's number. Carter took deep breaths, trying to calm the surge of adrenaline. Deepti was clearly still vibrating with it.

"Really, you can slow down," he said.

She blinked the wild look from her eyes and exhaled slowly through her nose, easing off the gas a little. She stole a look at Carter.

"I didn't think you were real."

Carter reloaded the spent shell from the shotgun. "Here I am."

"Not what I expected."

"Older, I bet."

"Yeah. By a lot."

Ivana called out from the backseat and told Deepti where the girls were.

"I know it," she said and took the next right turn. In a quarter mile, they had arrived at a grade school. Bree and Katie stood outside the only car in the lot next to a playground.

Carter pocketed the pistol and stowed the shotgun under the seat. He stayed back as mother and daughter had another tearful reunion. He got out and finally introduced himself to Deepti.

"I'm Carter."

"Deepti. And thank you. I guess I should have led with that."

"No need. Thanks for driving."

"I know where they're headed," she said.

"You do?"

"They talked a lot about a detention center near Tijuana at the border. I've read about it. They turn the people in for money and that's where they do it. Like a goddamn recycling center. Trade them in for cash."

"Okay. So I just need to make sure they don't get there."

"Yeah, if she goes in, the chances of getting her out are about zero. These clowns might be ICE cosplayers, but as soon as she gets down there, that's the real deal, and it's a goddamn fortress."

"Yeah, I've seen pictures."

Ivana came to him, her face tear-stained from hugging Katie. She threw her arms around Carter. "*Gracias. Muchas gracias.*"

He'd never been a hugger with anyone but his wife, but he took her embrace and squeezed her twice as hard.

"I'm sorry it took me so long."

When they parted, Bree was there. "You did it."

"Not all the way," he said. "There's more out there."

"Isla," she said.

"I'll be back."

Carter got back into his car. Deepti leaned into the window. "Let me come."

"No. No way."

"You got two guns. You can't take them alone."

"Not gonna happen."

He drove out of the lot. He reset the GPS back to the house, trying to come up with a plan for getting the rest of them out. One man was dead. A cop, which wasn't good. But if he was there trying to make bounty money off this scheme to exploit people, then he put himself in harm's way. And it hadn't been Carter's bullet that killed him.

The man he did shoot wore body armor. These men were ready. Carter had to be smart about it. When he got two blocks away, he had to relieve himself again. A fresh urgency hit him and would not be denied. He stopped behind a 7-11 and parked, leaving the car running. He unzipped and pissed against a wall. He saw more red. No time to deal with it now.

He finished up and got back in the car. He drove the two blocks and could see from down the street that the cube truck had gone.

Both bodies were missing from the yard. He surveyed the scene for a moment, sirens sounding from a distance but coming closer. A neighbor called it in, probably. That many gunshots wouldn't go unnoticed.

Carter drove away to meet up at the school again, a dull hum of pain vibrating through his gut. This current moved through him differently. Not the sharp ice pick stab he'd gotten used to over the past few months. This was like the neon glow of a beer sign in a bar window, buzzing red and constant. Better than the incapacitating slice through his midsection, but he hoped it would fade as quickly and not turn worse. He needed to hold on at least until Isla was safe. All he asked of his body was a few more hours.

Isla lay behind the seats of the truck on what was less a backseat and more a narrow bench for storage. She cried softly to herself as the men up front shouted over each other.

"What the fuck was that?" Luke wanted to know.

"*Who* was that?" Marco added.

MJ stared down at the gun in his hand. "Jesus Christ, Glenn…"

It was tight up front with four of them across the bench seat. Marco kept rubbing the spot where the bullet hit. He'd lived, but it still felt like he'd been punched with a sledgehammer. The vest had been little more than part of the costume, an accessory that made him feel badass. Now it had saved his life, so fuck that one guy on Facebook who had mocked his photo and called him a "Walmart Cop."

They'd lifted the two bodies into the back of the truck and left them there among the prisoners who all bunched together against the back wall. The man in black was behind the wheel, and he knew if they took any sharp corners, those bodies would slide around like loose groceries in the back.

"I didn't sign up for this shit," the man in black said.

"Shut up, Ian. You did, too," Marco said. "You took an oath."

"I took an oath in your kitchen, not to Homeland Security. Glenn is dead, man. So's that other dude."

MJ, on the far end of the bench against the door, whipped his head around to face Ian. "How'd you know about that?"

"Not that one," Luke said. "The guy with the foot."

"Wait, there's others?" Ian said. "Dammit."

Luke decided it was better not to tell him details about the man lying in a shallow grave out in the woods and just let it drop.

"So, what now?"

"South," Marco said. "Stick to the plan. Deliver this load, and we'll deal with the rest after that."

"That guy knows where I live."

"He got what he was after. Let him keep those two."

"I don't know, man."

"You got a better plan?"

Luke did not. He went quiet.

Behind him, Isla figured they forgot she was even there. They'd placed her in the cab of the truck hurriedly before they recovered the bodies from the front lawn. They packed up in a rush, expecting the police. If they showed up at the ICE facility with their payload, they were working for the government. A wild west shootout on Luke's front lawn would be harder to explain.

The man Ivana had told them about really did exist. He came to save her, like she said, but Isla had been left behind. What did she expect? She'd only known Ivana a short time, and the chances of her sending help were slim. Ivana got her rescue, and now Isla would become another statistic for Homeland Security quotas. Hot tears filled her eyes as the reality settled over her of never seeing Marta or her parents again.

A quartet of disappointed faces met Carter when he returned empty-handed. He explained how the truck had left by the time he got back to the house, and they set about making a plan.

"You said you know where they're going?"

"To the ICE detention center near San Diego," Deepti said. "I don't know exactly where, but it should be easy enough to find out."

"You look that up and then send me the location." Carter checked his gas gauge. Enough to get moving, but he'd need to stop by the time he reached LA.

"I'll ride with you then. The others can follow."

"No," he said. "I go alone."

All four women protested at once. He let them talk and ration out their arguments, but his resolve was firm. "I just got you out of harm's way," he said, looking at Ivana and then Deepti. "I'm not risking it again. We know they're capable of violence. I don't know how ugly this is gonna get."

Bree slapped her thigh in frustration. "I don't understand why we can't go to the police. We know about a truck full of people who've been kidnapped, basically."

"One of the guys with them was a cop," Carter said. "And half the guys posing as ICE are just cops on their day off. I wish it wasn't true, but right now, they're about the lowest on the list of who to trust with this."

"We have more than that on them," Deepti said. "And more than the dead bodies on the lawn."

"You've seen things?"

She worried over how much to say. "I don't know how it will incriminate me, or Isla, but a man who was with us in the garage got shot, and they made us bury him in the woods."

"Holy shit," Bree said.

"Yeah," Deepti said. "They held us at gunpoint and made us dig a grave. It was fucked up."

"They can't blame you for that."

"At this point, I don't even care. If it gets these bastards locked up, I'll tell the whole thing. I couldn't take them where it happened, though. Somewhere in Los Padres. They kept us in the dark."

"When all this shakes out, we'll decide if we need to use that. For now, I need to get moving. Chester, c'mon."

Chester hopped up from where he had been lying down and trotted over to Carter at the mention of his name.

"Wait, the dog gets to go, but not us?"

"That's the deal," Carter said. "Send me that info."

He held the door open for Chester, who climbed in the back seat. The old dog liked having a lower entry point than the old truck that Carter had to lift Chester in and out of. He'd need to stop and get some water, maybe something to eat along the way. He could fuel up at the same time, but every minute he waited, they were getting further South. He needed to pee again, too, but he didn't want to see the blood, so he put that off as well.

"Be careful," Bree said.

Katie said, "Good luck."

Deepti said, "This is bullshit."

Carter knew none of the women were happy about being left behind, but he'd risked their lives too much already. He did have an idea for some help, though. He hadn't wanted to say it in front of them and end up hearing about him asking for help from someone else, but when the thought came to him, he knew it would be the right call.

He scrolled his contacts, found the name, and punched the button. He pulled out of the parking lot, waving at Ivana as he left.

The phone answered after three rings. "You got Larry."

"Larry, this is Carter McCoy."

Larry was genuinely happy to hear from him. "Carter! How the hell are you?"

"Okay. Look, I need your help."

Carter explained the basics, leaving out the violence, his mistakes, and the danger involved.

"I figured maybe you'd have a much easier time tracking down one truck on a highway than I would."

"Right you are, my man," Larry said. "I'll put up the bat signal and get all the good ol' boys on the look-see. Most of these guys will be dying for something to do instead of just staring at the white lines."

"I appreciate it." He steered toward the highway headed South.

"Shit, I knew you were up to something interesting. But a goddamn rescue mission? Damn, son, that's some *Mission Impossible* shit right there."

"I don't know if I'd go that far."

"Rescuing people and shit? Yeah, that's something I can get behind. And fuck those ICE goons. That ain't my America."

Carter merged into the flow of southbound traffic. "How about your brethren? I bet there's a lot of truckers out there who are deep red."

"Too many, but there's plenty who know right from wrong."

"Well, I appreciate your help."

Larry asked about where they were last seen, and Carter explained.

"Shit, son, I'm right about on your front porch. I'm moving North back toward San Fran. I was about to drive right past you in two hours' time."

"Sorry I can't stop off and say hello, but I gotta try to cut them off if I can."

"I got you. I'll put the word out. Thanks for calling."

Carter hung up and merged left. He got into the fast lane and wondered if Chester counted for the carpool lane.

The dull throb in his gut lingered there like a tease. *I could split you in two and make it so you can't see straight, but I won't...yet.* It sat there like a heated coil, a reminder and a ticking clock.

Ivana hadn't let go of Katie since they saw each other. The tears finally stopped, but each one thought if they let go, the other might float away. It happened before, so they weren't taking chances.

Bree had been getting stories about what happened to Deepti, her jaw dropping further with each new tale.

"We should get back. You probably want to get home."

"What I want," Deepti said, "is to go after those fuckers."

"Carter can handle it."

"But why wouldn't more people be better? I get that he doesn't want anyone to run into harm's way, but I can make my own choices on that shit. And those fucking guys? Fuck them. This is my fight, not his."

Bree looked to Katie for some answers. She shrugged.

"I understand," Ivana said. "But he's only trying to protect us."

"Okay, very chivalrous of him, but did I ask for protection?"

The other three shuffled, finding it hard to disagree.

Deepti went on. "I don't have my car. I doubt if I even have a job after vanishing for so long. I should make a few phone calls, but all that can wait while those bastards are still out there and they still have Isla. If I could get in my own car and go, I would, but right now, I need a ride. What do you say?"

"I mean, yeah," Bree said. "Why not?"

Katie squeezed her mom's hand. "What do you think?"

"I think she's right. We came here to get Isla. That was the whole reason. Why are we stopping now?"

Bree had her phone out and pulled up her app where she could track Carter.

"He's going South on the one-oh-one."

"That girl needs our help," Deepti said. "And he might need us more than he thinks he does."

"Okay then," Ivana said. "Let's go."

They'd been driving South for a little over an hour, and the truck needed fuel. The men had gone quiet in the past half hour, drained and confused about next steps.

"I think after this, I'm gonna just apply for ICE," MJ said. "Make it official. They're paying great, I hear."

"You might have a little problem with the two people you shot," Luke said.

"I'm not gonna put that on my resume, obviously."

"Do you even realize how badly you've fucked up?"

MJ shifted in his seat to square off against Luke as much as he could. "Who put you in charge of this whole thing anyway?"

"I did! I brought you in. It was my goddamn idea, and on day one, I said nobody gets hurt."

"My mom always said you wanna make an omelette, you gotta break a few eggs."

Luke threw his hands up. "What the hell does that even mean?"

Marco banged on the dashboard three times, quickly. "Knock it off. Don't forget, Luke, I brought *you* in on this. I don't know which one of you fucked up, but somehow that guy knew where you were. You stop to think about that?"

Both men went quiet like little brothers put in their place.

"First," Marco said, "we need gas. Second, we gotta figure out where and how to dump those two bodies. You got a problem with that?"

"No," Luke said. "You don't think we should bring Glenn back with us? He's got family."

Marco gave him an "are you crazy?" look. "You wanna answer those questions? From the goddamn *cops?*"

"I'm just saying…"

"This thing is FUBAR. When that happens, you push on, and you move to the next task. Task one, gas. Task two, disposal. Task three, delivery and payment."

"Who gets Glenn's cut?" MJ asked.

Luke balled a fist and seriously considered punching him. This was his last run, for sure. And the last time he'd ever see MJ again. Let him go join ICE. Just get him the hell out of Luke's life.

"Gas station ahead, two miles," Ian said. He had kept his eyes on the road in a blank stare since they reached the highway. He wore a soldier's traumatized mask.

"Okay, good," Marco said. "Task one."

* * *

Isla lay quietly and listened. The steady movement of the truck had lulled her to sleep after the men went quiet, the exhaustion taking her down. Their argument had woken her up. She thought about escape strategies, but had no good ideas. She wondered about how she could alert another car on the highway, but had no way to do anything noticeable that wouldn't also get noticed inside the cab.

The helplessness covered her like heavy chains, and she wished she could sleep again.

Even a few miles inland from the beach, Carter marveled at how generic the landscape was. It wasn't the pine trees and lakes of Minnesota, but it wasn't the postcard beauty he attributed to California.

The sun had started to drop to the Western horizon. As he measured the days growing shorter while winter arrived, it all made sense to him. His entire world going dark alongside the world outside his small corner. Now these days, in the bright sunlight, no snow, no frost at night, no billows of his own breath when he walked outside, he felt the disconnect. The world would go on, even if his days kept getting shorter.

Chester always loved the steady hum of highway driving. He had curled himself into an awkward ball in the backseat of the compact car and had been snoring in a rhythmic pattern that worked Carter like a sleeping pill. He knew he would have to stop for a Coke soon. The car got great mileage, way better than his truck, but he should fill that up, too, so he could make it the rest of the way down to the border without stopping again.

As it got dark, finding the truck would be more difficult, if not impossible. But he had to try.

Experiencing so many setbacks and mistakes made him realize what a minor miracle his other missions had been. That he hadn't been caught by the police, that nobody else had been hurt other than his targets. That he somehow managed to come out alive.

Dumb luck, he figured.

If his luck held, he could bring Isla back. The ball of razors in his gut told him his luck was soon running out.

He pulled off the highway and into a gas station. Quaint by the massive truck stop standards of his cross-country drive. He filled up and left the pump running while he ran inside and got two bottles of Coke and three hot dogs from a spinning rack. One for him and two for Chester. He got some water, a Snickers bar, and a bag of almonds. He considered a beer, but chose against it.

He knew he'd be paying a cleaning fee when he turned in the rental, so he unwrapped the dogs and handed them over his shoulder to Chester, who ate each one in three gulping bites. Not even a crumb hit the upholstery. Maybe he could get away with a simple car wash vacuum.

He'd gotten an empty cup for a 32-oz soda and poured a water bottle into that for Chester. That went everywhere except for a small portion, which made it into his mouth.

Carter cracked the seal on his Coke with a hiss and pulled back onto the highway headed south with the sun racing toward the ocean.

In addition to the gas station, there was a chain burger place and a chain taco place. Ian guided the truck next to a pump carefully, checking that the top of the cube didn't scrape against the overhang. The men all slid out and stretched. They left Isla behind.

"Should we get them food?" Luke asked.

"How are we gonna give it to them?" Marco said. "Just roll up the back and let them take their pick?"

Luke increasingly became the odd man out. His partners didn't seem to think of their cargo as humans at all. If he were honest with himself, there was a time when he didn't either. Dollar amounts replaced names and faces in his mind when he began. But when they hung around longer, and when people started dying for this plan, he started to look at them differently.

"I tell you what," MJ said. "I'm gonna get a burger and take a leak."

"Sounds good," Marco said.

Ian kept quiet and went about the business of filling the tank.

"Can I use the bathroom?"

Luke looked up to see Isla leaning her head out the window of the passenger seat. He and MJ and Marco all traded a look, waiting for the others to make the call.

"I don't know, man," MJ said.

"I really need to go," she said.

An awkward beat of silence passed between the men as nobody wanted to commit. Finally, Luke said, "I'll take her."

The other two, happy to have the burden off of them, walked away toward the burger joint. Luke opened the door, and Isla climbed down. Her hands were still zip-tied in the front, and he quickly scanned the area to see if anyone was looking their way. He pulled out his pocketknife and clipped the plastic.

"No funny business," he said to her with the knife in hand.

"Yeah, okay."

He put a hand on her elbow and walked across the oil-stained blacktop toward the bathrooms. He let her go and tracked her like a security camera as she entered the Ladies' room. He stood sentry outside the door, peeking around the side to make sure there was no window she could climb out of. As soon as she had gone in, the urge to go himself hit. No way he was going in without her secure back in the truck, though. He put it out of his mind by thinking about the money he would get from his government and how the streets would be clean of more immigrant trash.

* * *

Ian counted the numbers climbing quickly. The pump chugged along at a syrupy-slow pace. He could squeeze the handle and make it go a little faster, but he leaned against the side of the truck and let the automatic flow creep along.

A loud thump sounded behind him, and he jumped. Then a voice, muffled but urgent, came from inside the truck. He unfolded his arms and turned to face the stained white cargo cube of the truck. Another thud, then four more in rapid succession. Then a chorus of voices shouting in Spanish, with an occasional word in English, cutting through.

Shit. This was bad.

Ian spun toward a woman filling her SUV while staring at the truck and trying to discern the source of the noises she heard. He cursed to himself, "Shit, shit, shit." He tried coughing to cover the noise, but the pounding now sounded like a hailstorm had broken out inside the truck.

A man walked from the burger place with a paper bag already dark with grease stains and a paper cup of soda. He eyed the truck, then Ian. He paused.

"Everything all right?"

"Yeah," Ian said. "Moving some shit and got some loose furniture back there. My buddies are trying to tie it down."

"Oh yeah?" He sipped his drink, but didn't move.

"Yeah. I think one of them stubbed his toe." Ian banged his fist on the side three times and then shouted, "Come on, guys, hurry it up in there." He offered a weak smile to the man.

The pounding continued, a sloppy, mistimed drum solo. The steel walls of the truck muted the shouting so the words didn't come through clearly, but the sentiment did. Ian felt an itch pull him toward the gun in the cab. He reached for the pump handle and cut off the flow. Only about six gallons had gone in, but he wanted out.

The man with the bag moved along, turning his neck as he walked to keep an eye on Ian and the truck.

Ian hung the handle and shuffled away toward the building.

The man with the bag made it across the lot to his semi truck waiting for him. He hauled himself up into the cab, set his bag on the seat beside him, and picked up the handset for his CB radio. "Larry, you out there?"

A crackle of static and then, "You got him."

"What was the plate on the truck you were looking for?"

* * *

"We gotta go," Ian said. He didn't care who heard him. Marco and MJ were still in line waiting for their food, and Ian held the door open across the busy burger joint.

"We don't have our food yet," Marco explained.

"We gotta move. Now."

Ian's shuffling footsteps and panicked demeanor told them this was serious. Marco moved first, and MJ followed. They left behind their burgers still on the grill and followed Ian outside.

On their way back to the truck, Ian called to Luke, who waited outside the restrooms.

"We're leaving. Right now. Let's go."

All three men jogged by. Something had gone seriously wrong. For a brief moment, Luke considered leaving Isla behind. If something had happened to panic the others, then time was of the essence. But he considered how much she could tell somebody about them. About him. She may have been a burden to carry with them, but she was more of a liability on her own.

He opened the Ladies' Room door and shouted, "We're leaving. Move it."

"Gimmie a minute," she replied.

"Now!"

By the time they reached the truck, Ian had the engine idling. Gripping her tight by the elbow, Luke helped guide Isla back into the cab of the truck. She climbed over the seat into the back bench area.

He could clearly hear the clattering from inside the truck as they made their way over. They'd attracted a small crowd. The woman with the SUV, two men in coveralls, and an older man in a plaid shirt.

"Get in, get in," Marco urged him. Luke pulled the door closed behind him, and Ian had dropped the truck in gear before it was shut.

"What the hell is going on?"

"It's them," Marco said, throwing a crooked thumb over his shoulder at the back of the truck.

Ian made a sharp swerve as he exited the lot. Luke knew it was on purpose. And he knew that the people in back would lose their balance and slip to the floor, probably colliding with the two dead bodies back there. But it worked, and the banging stopped.

"Last stop," Marco said. "We keep going from here."

"I didn't get to piss," MJ said.

"Piss out the window."

Ian pointed at the instrument panel. "We only got like a quarter tank. I had to pull it early."

"God dammit." Marco punched the black plastic dashboard.

Behind them on the bench, Isla smiled to herself.

Carter pressed SCAN on the radio, and the numbers climbed until it
landed on a signal. Nothing Carter knew. After a few seconds, it continued
on and landed on a song that sounded exactly the same to him. Three more
stops up the dial and nothing that sounded much like music to Carter, so he
snapped off the radio.

The sun had gone, but a dull glow held on to the West. Headlights sped
past, headed north on the highway, looking like comets burning up in the
atmosphere. When the sun went down, every state looked the same. He
could be driving under the ocean for all he knew.

He kept his speed right under 75. Fast enough to hopefully gain on the
truck, but not fast enough to attract the police.

Carter hated how sad it made him that he had come to distrust men and
women in uniform. He lamented what this country had become, like the
fabled "big one" had hit and cut the nation right in two down a fault line,
splitting empathy and greed. Fear and anger had taken over for reason and
thought. Truth had become subjective, and nobody listened anymore. All
that was far more troubling to him than some songs he no longer recognized.

His phone buzzed in the cup holder where he had it stowed. He lifted it
and did his best to keep one eye on the road. He expected Bree or Ivana, but
it was Larry. He thumbed the answer button and then speaker.

"Hey there."

Larry was excited and shouted like he was speaking over the noise of a jet
engine. "Carter! We got 'em."

"What? You did?"

"Buddy of mine spotted them at a gas station. Said there were sounds coming from the truck like people inside wanting real bad to get out."

"I'll be damned."

"I'm turning around. They're real close. Just a little south."

Larry gave Carter a mile marker and the name of the town where his buddy had spotted the truck. Carter kept an eye on the side of the highway, looking for a mile marker to figure out how far away he was.

"Chuck's on their tail. He's gonna stick with 'em until I catch up. I told him what's what, and he wants to bust these boys."

"Amazing. Let him know they're armed and dangerous. He can follow, but tell him not to get too close. I'll figure out where I am in relation and hopefully catch up soon."

"Ten-four. I'll be right on your tail." Larry giggled like he was enjoying all this. "Hot damn, a real live chase. Carter, I'm damn glad I picked you up."

"Look, I don't think I can do this."

Ian wouldn't turn his head to look at the hard stares coming his way. He kept his eyes forward toward the highway, but they were anything but focused on the road.

"What the hell does that mean?" Marco asked.

"Just means I don't want to do this anymore. I'm out."

"You can't be out. We're all in this together."

Ian squeezed the wheel tight with both hands. "No, man. I'm done. I'm not down with this shit anymore." He flipped the indicator and merged right, angling toward the next exit.

"What the hell are you doing, dude?" MJ said.

"Drop me off. I'll get a ride back. But fuck this, I'm out." He guided the truck into the far right lane.

"Ian, don't be stupid," Marco said.

"Hey, if he quits," MJ said, "We split his cut."

"Do what you want," Ian said. "I don't want the money."

The truck eased onto an off-ramp. Marco punched the dashboard. "God DAMN it."

"Let him go," Luke said. "If he's not into it, he's a liability."

"So, three way split?" MJ said.

Ian still wouldn't look to his right other than to check the mirror. Marco was close enough he could feel his breath on his neck.

"What if I think you know too much to just split without a little insurance?"

"What the hell does that mean?" Ian asked.

"You know what's in the back of the truck. You know what went down at Luke's house. How do I know you won't go to the cops or something?"

"Because I was there, too. Shit, that's why I'm getting out. I'm too deep in this already, and I want nothing to do with it. I'm getting out because… because…because fuck this shit."

He angled the truck toward an In-N-Out Burger parking lot.

"Yeah, don't forget that you were there. Anything happens to us, yours is the first name out of my mouth. You were the ringleader. You pulled the trigger."

"Fuck you, that was MJ."

"Not anymore, it's not. That's my insurance, so don't get cute."

"This is some high-level bullshit, man."

When Ian opened the door to climb out, a waft of French fry grease and burning beef patties filled the cab. A long line of cars snaked through the lot, and two teenagers in white outfits leaned in windows to take orders. Ian left the truck running and the door open as he walked away.

Marco called after him, "Don't try to come back and get in on this for the next one. You're done, man. Fuckin' traitor."

"Screw you, Marco." Ian raised a middle finger over his head as he walked away, not looking back.

"Forget it," MJ said. "This is good news. Three ways is better than four ways, right?"

Marco slid over into the driver's seat. "Yeah, I guess."

"I think we should get rid of the bodies," Luke said. "The longer we have them, the riskier it is. Someone wants to ask questions about the people; we got the power of the President behind us. Dead bodies, though?"

"Yeah. Probably best. We gotta get away from the highway, though. East, into the scrub."

"We don't have shovels or anything."

"We just gotta get creative about where we dump them. I'll find a service road. All we need is a few days. Coyotes will get rid of them. Maybe even mountain lions."

"There's no goddamn mountain lions around here," MJ said.

"Yes, there are. Bears, too. Big fuckers."

Luke nodded. "No, he's right. If we get even a little way into the hills, we have a good shot at something like that."

Marco put the truck in gear.

"Hold it," MJ said. "As long as we're here, I'm gonna pee and get a burger."

"Yeah, good call." Marco drove the truck to the far corner of the lot in case the people in back wanted to get loud again.

"I'll stay here," Luke said. "Get me a double-double."

Marco and MJ got out, leaving Luke alone on the bench seat. Luke put his head in his hands, enjoying the momentary quiet. This whole thing had gotten out of hand. A few dollars on the side, a way to make America great again and fight the scourge of illegal aliens had become blood on his hands, cover-ups and fleeing the scene. And he hadn't even gotten paid yet. How could his President stiff him on payment? Probably some Democrat in Congress holding things up, but still...

"Nothing for me?"

Luke jolted at the voice. He jerked his head around so fast his muscles tightened, and he winced. He'd forgotten Isla was there.

"Jesus Christ."

"I'm hungry too, you know."

Luke exhaled, trying to slow his racing pulse. "You can have half of mine."

"Never mind. I guess they'll feed us when we get there."

"Probably."

"Do you even know what those places are like?"

Luke didn't, but he'd never admit it. "Should have thought about that before you came here."

"I was *born* here, dumbass." She sighed. "You didn't listen the first fifty times, why should you listen now?"

"If you're legit, they'll sort you out."

Isla leaned forward and rested her elbows on the back of the bench seat. "You ever hear innocent until proven guilty? No, I doubt it. All you guys love to talk about the Constitution, but I doubt any of you have ever read it."

"Bullshit."

"What's the Fifth Amendment?"

Luke's mouth hung open, but no sound came out.

"How about the ninth?"

He closed his mouth.

Isla leaned back. "I thought so."

* * *

MJ veered left when they got close to the burger place.

"Where are you going?" Marco asked.

"You aren't really gonna let him leave, are you?"

Marco noticed MJ's hand in his pocket. He knew MJ's fist was wrapped around his gun.

"Yeah, I am."

"C'mon, man. He knows too much."

Marco squared off, feet set apart, hands girding his loins. "What do you plan to do about it?"

MJ shrugged. "Y'know…"

"No, I don't. Enlighten me."

"Make sure he can't talk."

Marco took two steps closer to MJ, leaned in close. "You're one whacked-out individual, you know that? Take your hand out of your pocket, go inside and order some food, take a piss, and then we're leaving. Whatever Ian wants to do is his business. He won't talk. I trust him."

"Yeah, you trust him. I barely know him. How am I supposed to trust him?"

"That's what the money's for."

The two men continued on into the In-N-Out. MJ's head hung low. Idling nearby was a semi truck. Behind the wheel, a man watching them intently.

Carter's phone rang.

"They stopped again," Larry said. "Getting food, looks like." He told Carter the details and mile marker of the exit they'd taken. "You'll see the sign from the highway."

"Okay. By the mile markers, I'm about ten miles behind."

"This oughta catch you up a bit then."

"Good." Carter pressed down a little more on the accelerator, breaking past his seventy-five-mile-an-hour limit.

"I'm behind about fifty, but on my way."

"Great. Thanks, Larry."

They hung up with promises to meet up soon. Carter set a hand on top of Chester's head and let it rest there. The burning in his gut hadn't subsided. It was a constant heat now, sitting somewhere below his stomach, pressing into his spine.

Darkness spread out from either side of the highway. No towns nearby on this stretch. He hadn't fully realized how long California was, nor how much of it was empty. All he ever heard about were the cities. Here, along the central coast, much of it remained wild and open. Hills rising to the East on his left and the slow dip toward the ocean to the West on his right.

When all this was over, he really needed to see the beach.

"What do you say, boy?" He rubbed his hand along Chester's head until his ears flopped. "Gotta see the ocean at least once, right?"

He ran over images in his head of things he'd seen, places he'd been. Running an inventory of a life lived. He tried not to dwell on the places he wouldn't see. Paris, Japan, an African safari. He'd never been up to Alaska or out as far as Maine. He'd never tried water skiing or flown first class or eaten sushi. The *never-have* list grew much longer. It was true of about anyone, he supposed.

Carter had a different list of things he had done than most men. He'd killed in cold blood. He'd fought to defend himself and others. He'd lost a child. Items on a list he wouldn't wish on anyone.

And then bigger items, more important and more memorable than any sight he'd ever seen or place he'd ever been. The love of a good woman. The joy of raising a child. The company of a good dog.

He could trade Paris for that. Hell, he could trade walking on the moon for that.

"If this ends and we have anything left in the tank," he said to Chester. "Maybe I'll get a tattoo."

Chester grumbled, probably hungry.

"Not for you, buddy. Just me."

The other cars kept pace as he pushed it up over eighty. Along the black highway, limits didn't seem to matter anymore. Clusters of light cropped up on one side of the highway or the other, but he passed them quickly, and the surrounding landscape faded to black again.

Only pinpoints of light from oncoming headlights. A scattering of stars overhead. A slow draining of all light in the world. It had been his world since the diagnosis. A clock ticking toward midnight. A road running to the end of land, to the limit of how far he could go.

Bree drove. Ivana and Katie sat together in back, holding hands. Deepti rode up front, keeping an eye on every exit sign, every mile marker, and indication of where they were. On the console between them, Bree's phone was open to the tracking app showing Carter's car as a blue dot moving steadily south on the 101 freeway.

"I wish we could track Isla with this thing," Deepti said.

"Yeah, I know."

Bree had made another call to Mrs. Borgeson to check on Marta. Mrs. B had her in front of the TV, eating a take-out pizza. "She's been through enough," she said. "She can have whatever she wants." Bree didn't argue.

"Y'know, I worried it would come to this," Deepti said. "I didn't really think it would, though."

"Yeah, I wish Carter had been able to get all three of you out."

"Not just that." Deepti kept her eyes focused out the window, searching the dark for signs they were getting close. "The whole country. I never wanted to be doom and gloom, even when I was worried. But this shit is worse than I expected."

"What's that thing, the arc of history?"

"Bends toward justice, yeah. But also, you ever see how empires fall? Kinda feels like we're on the downslide, doesn't it?"

"All I care about right now is getting Isla back home safe."

"I'm with you on that. I'd also like to fuck those guys up a little bit, if I'm honest."

"Yeah. That'd be good, too."

Deepti checked the app again. "Says he's going eighty now. Wonder if he saw something that made him speed up?"

Bree checked her own speedometer, sitting at seventy-eight. She didn't want to push it much more, even though the traffic around her flowed at the same rate, and now and then, they still got passed.

"If we're lucky, he found them."

"Unlucky for them."

The cube truck swayed and rattled down the 101. Cars passed, headed home or out on some journey, semi trucks roared by delivering goods, none of them had any idea they'd passed nearly a dozen prisoners and two dead bodies in the back of the nondescript truck.

"How about here?" Marco pointed at an exit surrounded by darkness.

"Let's try it," Luke said.

Marco eased the truck over and slipped off the highway. Once off, he turned left, passed back under the highway, and moved East toward darkened hills.

"What is this, Los Padres?" Luke asked.

"Yeah, I think so."

"Should be some access roads around."

They moved past two stop signs, and the surrounding traffic faded away. They began to climb into an area where nobody bothered to put up street lights. Where the road had no painted lines. The truck angled up, and they rose into the foothills, unaware of the semi truck that had pulled off behind them.

* * *

Carter answered his phone.

"They got off the highway," Larry said, and he gave him the exit number. "Chuck said they turned up into the hills. He had to stop and wait; otherwise, they'd see him for sure. These rigs ain't exactly discreet."

Carter scanned the road signs. Only one exit away. "Where do you think they're going?"

"No idea. There's nothing around there I know of."

"Hmmm."

Carter signaled and started to make his way right toward the exit.

* * *

A tall tower on a nearby hill blinked a red beacon, and Marco aimed for that.

They were alone in the deep black. A half-moon lit short trees and deep crevices where the hills had been pushed up by the edge of the continent, crunched and crinkled like used tinfoil in someone's fist.

"How are we gonna bury them?" MJ asked.

"Can't," Marco said. "Gotta dump them and give a little cover. Out of sight just in case anyone came by. Predators will find them by the smell. As long as we leave them exposed enough that the critters can get to them, they'll be nothing but bones in a week."

An involuntary shudder twitched across Luke's shoulders like a spider's legs scurrying across the floor. "Jesus."

"It's gotta be done."

"I guess."

Luke was glad he gave half his burger to Isla. Being weighed down by a double patty of greasy hamburger meat while he was trying to dispose of two bodies that had been cooking in the back of the truck for several hours wasn't exactly appetizing.

Marco flipped on his brights and angled the truck up a side road that faded quickly into inky black ahead of them. Insects buzzed the bright lights like snow flurries. MJ powered down his window and tossed his empty soda cup out into the dark. A moth got inside the cab and immediately regretted the choice. Panicked flapping and slamming into the windshield and the roof ensued. MJ buzzed up the window and slapped a flat palm against the dashboard, flattening the moth. He wiped his hand across his pant leg and let out a belch.

* * *

Carter pulled alongside the idling semi truck waiting on the side of a cracked-pavement access road. But access to what, Carter didn't know. Who needed access to this nothingness?

"Chuck?"

Chuck shoved his mesh ball cap back on his head, turned off the rumbling engine. "You Larry's pal?"

"Yeah. Carter. Thanks for your help."

"My pleasure. Sounds like a real set of assholes you're tracking."

"You could say that."

Chester woke up momentarily and sniffed at the open window, then went back to his nap.

Chuck looked toward the rising hill in front of them. "Wish my rig could make it up there, but I don't do hills so good."

"You're good. You see which way they went?"

Chuck pointed into the darkness. "Straight through, then I saw taillights head right where it goes up. Just follow that tower light there, and you'll be headed the right way."

Chuck indicated the same blinking red light Marco had followed. Only one way up. Not a lot of cross streets out in the National Forest.

Carter nodded. "Really appreciate it. Take care."

Carter continued up the road and made his first right, following the trail up into the black hills. He had them on the line, reeling them in slowly, ready for a showdown.

The ground leveled out, and Marco was sick of driving anyway.

"This'll do."

He eased the truck off the road and onto the pine-needle-covered ground of a small clearing. He put it in park and left the engine idling.

Luke eyed the rim of light from the headlamps outside, the line of trees, the lack of any evidence of humans ever being here. "Yeah, looks good enough."

Marco got one foot out the door and aimed a thumb over his shoulder at the bench behind them. "Grab her, and we'll finally put her in back with the others."

MJ got out the other side, and Luke turned to Isla apologetically. "Come on," he said.

As soon as he was out and on the ground, MJ's gun came out. He swiveled his head left and right, checking the tree line for anyone lurking or for bears, maybe mountain lions. Marco made his way to the back gate and flipped the latch. "Ready?"

MJ adjusted his grip on the gun. "Yep."

Luke stood off to the side, his hand on Isla's elbow. The heavy black hole of the dark woods in front of her like the absence of hope, the long stretch of empty road, seeming to fade into oblivion, and all ideas of making a run for it vanished. Escape out into that void, and she'd be dead within two days.

"We don't have a flashlight or something?" Luke asked.

The headlights provided a dull glow around them, but with most of the light aimed the other direction, the rear of the truck remained very dark. Marco and MJ didn't have a response and stared, dumbfounded, at each other.

"I got a flashlight on my phone," MJ said. He withdrew his phone and held it in his left hand, unwilling to relinquish his gun for a little light. When he powered on the flashlight, it cast a weak cone of light directly in front of him, but nothing you'd call bright.

"What about the flare?" Marco said. Without waiting for an answer, he went back to the cab, dug into the roadside assistance kit beneath his seat, and came back with a short red stick. He removed the cap, scratched the lighter across the tip, and the forest was cast in a deep red glow. The hiss from the flare filled the space as fully as the light.

"Careful with the pine needles," Luke said. "We don't want to start a fire."

Marco raised the flare higher and mocked him, "Okay, Smokey the bear."

Marco lifted the back gate. Four of the men inside were right there, waiting to pounce. They took in the eerie glow from the flare, the gun in MJ's hand, Isla being held tight – and froze.

"No funny stuff," Marco said. "All we want are the bodies."

The men looked like they'd been stuffed into a bag and shaken. Luke could make out the dim outlines of the women's faces huddled against the back wall of the truck, made all the more frightened-looking by the red glow casting deep shadows into the belly of the truck. He'd seen the images of immigrants coming here illegally and what they often had to endure. Heartless coyotes, putting them through torture in cramped spaces and denied water and basic services to reach their American dream. Seeing it in person made him wonder why anyone would endure such a thing. Whatever they were running from must be worse, but how could it be?

He shook off the unfamiliar feeling of empathy. They were just here to suck at the teat of American entitlement programs. To leech off his taxes and steal his government services. They deserved what they got. Didn't they?

One of the men had a cut across his forehead that bled down across his face, leaving dried streaks of blood that turned black in the flare's glow.

"Get 'em down," Marco commanded. The men didn't argue. They were glad to be rid of the corpses they'd been riding companions with for a hundred miles.

Bree glanced at the dashboard and realized she'd been doing ninety. She hadn't noticed until she passed a fifth and sixth car to her right. Her anxious foot had kept pushing down a little bit more with each passing mile. She let off a bit and coasted for a while.

"Looks like he got off the highway," Deepti said.

Bree took her eyes off the road to glance at her phone screen, where the app showed Carter's little blue dot moving East into a vast blank area on the map.

"Where's he going?"

"I don't know, but we're going to the same place." Deepti lifted the phone and pinched her fingers to zoom in on the screen. "Holy shit, he's right ahead."

Bree changed lanes and got ready to take the exit. She braked and slid in behind a slow-moving pickup truck laden with boxes.

"I hope he's okay with us following him," Ivana said.

"Why wouldn't it be okay with some backup?" Deepti asked.

"How are we going to back him up? With what?"

Deepti looked from the screen out into the night. "I'll tell you what I'm gonna use—my furious fucking anger."

Bree reached the far right lane and pushed the car back up over eighty-five, eyes out for the exit sign.

Carter drove slowly up the switchbacks and inclines. There weren't intersecting streets or options for where the truck could turn off and lose him. He kept it slow and steady, knowing he'd reach them eventually. As soon as he held some confidence that the single-lane road would lead him to where he needed to go, the road split. He came to a stop, and Chester sat up, thinking they'd reached their destination.

"Not yet, bud," Carter said.

He studied the road in the headlight glow and looked for some indication of which way the truck had gone. He looked up to try to see the blinking beacon, but the trees were too dense around him.

Chester whined.

"Yeah, you probably need to go out, huh?"

Carter could use a bathroom break, too. He clipped Chester's leash and let him step down gently from the car. He walked forward, into the pool of light made by the headlights, and let Chester sniff. That dog could hunt down any manner of critter on four legs, but Carter wished he could track a white cube truck right then.

Chester made it to the trees and sniffed up the side of one as high as his nose would reach. Squirrel, perhaps? Possum? Raccoon? Maybe all three. Whatever it was, Chester was loving the buffet of new smells. Chester lifted his leg and marked his presence for them to smell when the critters returned. A greeting card from Minnesota.

Carter looped the leash around his wrist and stepped up to the tree to make his own mark. His bladder gripped like a ball of hot wax, and his urine burned on the way out. Carter sucked air through his teeth. He didn't need to see to know there was blood; he could feel it.

He finished and let Chester mark three more trees before tugging at the leash to turn him around.

"C'mon, we gotta pick which way to go. Wish I had a coin to flip."

Chester's nose caught on some new scent, and he pulled to the right. Carter's feet crossed over one another, and he nearly went down. "Damn it, Chester."

When he righted himself, he saw that Chester was sniffing at an In-N-Out cup with its red palm trees on a white background. The writing on the logo matched the roadside sign he'd seen at the exit Chuck had said they turned off. The cup looked new, too, not weathered and broken down like something that had been there in the elements for a while.

When Carter turned back to see where the car was behind them, he could tell they'd wandered about thirty feet down the side road, and Carter knew which way the truck had turned.

He patted Chester on the head. "Good boy."

The second body landed on the ground. It was stiff and didn't bend at first, but when it hit, the full weight of Glenn, the former cop, folded over on itself and then came to a rest on top of a bed of pine needles.

"Hey, careful goddammit," Marco said. "That was a friend of ours."

The men in the truck held up their hands and backed away into the shadow of the cube truck. Marco continued to hold the flare aloft and light the area in a glow like a giant neon beer sign had been left on.

"What now?" MJ asked.

"We gotta stash them."

MJ pointed the gun toward the open truck. "Make them do it."

"They could run."

MJ looked around at the dark trees surrounding them. "Where?"

"I don't fucking know, but we shouldn't risk it."

"Well, I don't want to move around a couple of dead bodies."

Marco faced MJ, the flare burning angrily between them. "Then you shouldn't have fucking shot them."

Luke wondered if maybe making a run for it was a good idea. The more time he spent with these two, the more he wanted to be anywhere else. The two men they'd lost meant his share of the money went up, but the faces of the men and women inside the truck were getting to him. And Isla in his grip, what had she done? She kept saying she was a citizen. Maybe it was true.

He knew he couldn't run off into the forest, but as soon as they dropped off this load at the ICE detention, he needed to break away. Maybe he'd take one of those offers to become a real ICE agent. The money was damn good, and they operated pretty much above the law. But it was probably filled with guys like MJ, not guys like Luke, who only wanted to make the country better and more pure. Misdirected anger and bitterness with a fresh target in these people, just trying to make a better life for themselves. People had died at the hands of these agents. MJ would fit right in.

"We don't have shovels anyway," he said. "Just leave them there and let's go."

"We have to hide them a little bit," Marco said. "You can see them from the road."

"Who the hell even comes up here?"

As if he'd summoned them, a pair of headlights swept through the trees.

Carter had spotted the red glow from far off. It was hard to judge how close he was to it. The hills themselves seemed to be emitting the ball of red light, like the open mouth of a volcano had somehow opened in the foothills of central California.

Thinking he was close enough, he pulled to the side.

"You stay here," he said to Chester.

Carter reached for the shotgun and dug the box of shells from the glove box. He put the pistol in his pocket and got out, cracking a window slightly for Chester.

He could pee again, but he held it. Pissing blood only reminded him of how unqualified he was as a rescue force of one. Isla needed Rambo. She was getting Carl from *Up*. But he would give all he had to give.

As mild as the temperatures had been all week, the hills at night brought a chill. It made him feel at home and gave him a surge of energy. He walked toward the glow.

* * *

Chuck had been frustrated by the lack of signal for his cell phone. He'd been tracking several eBay auctions in order to add to his collection of vintage Matchbox cars. Ever since his mother had thrown out his childhood keepsakes, he'd been obsessed with buying back as many as he could get his hands on, as long as they were pre-1990. He killed time listening to CDs while waiting for the old man to come back down the mountain. He didn't dare leave until he knew the conclusion to this weird manhunt he'd been dragged into.

Headlights caught his mirrors as another semi truck approached from behind.

Larry pulled next to him, and the two men spoke to each other through their rolled-down windows, as if each were still connected to their trucks like a permanent fixture.

"You see Carter come through?"

"Yeah," Chuck said. "He followed them up that way."

Larry studied the road that climbed into darkness. "No way my rig is gonna make it up there."

"Yeah, I didn't want to risk it."

Larry kept his eyes forward, wishing he could go. "Damned exciting, isn't it?"

"It's something different, that's for damn sure."

Another set of headlights appeared in Larry's mirrors. A small hatchback came to a stop beside Larry's truck. Ivana leaned out the window.

"Hello, Larry."

"Ivana!"

"Is Carter here?"

"He's up there." Larry pointed ahead. "Came by…what?" He turned to Chuck, who said, "Maybe ten minutes ago."

"Think we can find the way?"

Chuck leaned out his window and shouted so the car of women could hear him. "If you follow that flashing beacon…" When he pointed, he noticed the far-off red glow of the flare. "Hang on a minute."

Larry followed his eyes. "I see it. What is that? Tail lights?"

"Maybe. Pretty far up there."

"Gotta be them, though."

Bree leaned forward over the steering wheel to see the light they were talking about.

Larry got out of his cab. "Can I ride with you? My rig won't make it too far up that hill."

"Yes, of course," Ivana said. Looking at Katie and the small space in back. "Maybe you should wait here."

"Are you serious, Mom?" They were no longer in a life and death hunt for a missing girl; they were mother and daughter disagreeing at the kitchen counter like a hundred times before. "I'm not letting you go toward the danger and staying behind. Never again. If anything you should stay behind. You've been through enough, but I don't even want to leave you here because I don't want to lose sight of you."

"I know, but–"

"You've taught me a lot of stuff, Mom. Not just recipes and things like that, but, like, real things. How to be strong and how to face the danger. I'm not sitting on the sidelines now."

"Tell her, girl," Deepti said from the front.

"You're right." Ivana laid a hand on Katie's cheek. "You're not my baby girl anymore."

She slid closer to Katie and made room for Larry in back.

"You can take off, Chuck," Larry said.

"No way," Chuck said. "I gotta see how this plays out."

Larry closed the door, introductions were made, and Bree started up the hill.

The trees glowed as if they were on fire. Carter crept closer, trying to make out shapes in the blood-red haze of the flare light. He could see the truck. He made out two shapes near the rear bumper, bodies perhaps. He saw nobody else. Not Isla, not the men.

He stopped and crouched to one knee. Maybe a mistake. Standing up from any low position wasn't as easy as it once was for him.

The flare leaned at an angle on the shapes that may have been bodies. As Carter's eyes adjusted to the light, he confirmed that they were. The flare had been wedged into the back pocket of one of the two corpses. It hissed its way past halfway, burned up.

The back gate of the truck stood open, the light not quite penetrating inside, making a dull black hole in the sea of red. A tentative movement, then a face appeared. The man was worried, peering out like a rodent on the lookout for predators. The flare caught the edges of his features and made him a stark relief of shadows and dark angles.

Another face appeared next to him, then a third. They ventured to the edge of the truck's back gate and looked out into the clearing. Words were exchanged that Carter could not hear, and one man put a hand on the support handle and moved to lower himself out of the truck.

From around the side came MJ with his gun out and threatening.

"Not so fast, Pedro. Back inside."

The three faces disappeared back into the shadow of the truck.

From the other side of the truck came Marco, clad in his camouflage, the dark circle of Carter's bullet hit still marring the front of his shirt.

"You see anyone?" he asked.

"Nope," MJ said.

Two men isolated. Carter wasn't going to get a better chance. He had to decide: give them another chance to give up the hostages or make them pay? They'd had one chance already, and they chose to shoot. They would have killed him, he knew. They did kill one of the hostages, and according to Deepti, there had been others before. Men like that deserved punishment.

As he feared, standing didn't come easily. He pushed up, and the bed of old pine needles rustled under him. Both men turned his way. Carter lifted the shotgun and fired.

He kept his shot low so no buckshot would spread into the open mouth of the truck. Dirt, dead leaves, and pine needles kicked up, but neither man was hit. They both moved swiftly, retreating back around opposite sides of the truck. MJ flung his arm out and fired a wild shot behind him just as he had back in the front yard, where Carter first found them. Not a threat for his strategy and cunning, but still a threat for his recklessness.

Carter moved to his right, keeping a layer of trees between him and the clearing. The sudden adrenaline surge had his bladder bursting.

* * *

"Stay here," Luke said.

He'd retreated into the cab of the truck with Isla. He slid out, and as he shut the door behind him, he drew his own gun for the first time this trip. Somehow, the madman from his front lawn had found him.

MJ came scrambling around the corner of the truck and fell onto his knees as he ducked into safety. He spun and faced back toward the clearing with his gun outstretched, searching the shadows for the shooter. A half grin crept along the edges of his mouth.

"What the hell was that?" Luke asked.

"Someone shot at us."

"Did you get him?"

"I don't know."

Luke crouched next to MJ and moved his eyes along the tree line, looking for signs of movement, but seeing only darkness devouring the flare light, which had started to dim as the flare burned down.

"How the fuck did he find us?" Luke asked.

"How the hell should I know?"

A sound drew their attention, and each man held his breath as they listened. A thump, then shuffling of feet. Both men leaned out to get a better look into the clearing. The sound repeated, then again, and again.

Luke could see silhouetted shapes moving in the glow, but not their shooter. Another person jumped down from the truck and landed on the pine needle carpet.

"God dammit," MJ said. "They're getting away."

He stood and raised his gun.

Luke shouted to him, "What the hell are you doing?"

"They're running."

The last of the women jumped from the back of the truck. The men each grabbed the hand of a woman and pulled them along as the group of ten all ran in different directions.

MJ fired.

The mad scramble sounded like a flock of birds taking off. Muttered Spanish, urging the slower ones along, floated above the scrape of feet along the forest floor.

"You can't shoot them," Luke said.

"Look at them," MJ said before firing again at the shadows in the glow. "They're running."

No bodies fell. Pairs of shapes split off from one another and aimed for cover in the trees.

Luke stood behind MJ. "Fuckin' stop shooting."

"That's my goddamn money."

A shot rang out, but MJ hadn't pulled the trigger. He went stiff, then clutched at his chest. He put a hand on his sternum and touched blood still warm from his body. Luke stood behind him, point-blank range, with a gun trembling at the end of his outstretched arm. A dark stain spread across

MJ's back where the bullet had gone in. The smaller hole in front, where the bullet exited, leaked blood through MJ's fingers.

MJ turned and recognized Luke, but didn't understand. A question unanswered hung between them. A twisted confusion faded from his face as a slack-jawed blankness took over. MJ dropped his precious gun, fell to his knees, then forward onto his face.

Luke lowered his gun as the retreating shadows of the captives vanished into the trees.

"Another one," Deepti said.

They'd parked behind Carter's car as the first shotgun blast rang out. Quickly after, the other shots had come.

"What do we do?" Bree said.

"Carter might be in trouble," Ivana said.

Larry made a show of patting his pockets. "God damn. Left my gun behind."

Chester sat with his ears forward, head tilted slightly as he pressed his nose against the window.

"We have to help him," Bree said.

Deepti turned to Ivana. "You stay here with your daughter. Keep an eye on those trees. I'm going."

Ivana held both of Katie's hands. "Is that okay with you?"

"I'm not leaving you. It's my turn to keep you safe."

"Okay." She turned to Deepti. "If anyone comes this way, we will try to stop them."

"You got the car. Fucking run them over."

Bree peered into Carter's rental car. "Keys are in this one, too."

"There you go," Deepti said. "Two weapons at your disposal." She moved off toward the red glow and the fading sounds of the gunshots. Bree followed on her heels.

"Damn, woman," Larry said. "You're something else." He fell in behind them.

Katie called after them, "Be careful."

The clatter of footsteps sounded like a herd of deer racing through the woods. Bree slid behind a tree. Larry reached out and pulled Deepti close to him, and put them both behind a tree. The unexpected sight of nearly a dozen men and women running out of the darkness made Deepti suck in a breath and hold it.

In pairs, some holding hands, the runners made for the road, shifting and moving around trees and avoiding running in a straight line as if they were dodging enemy fire on the front lines.

Deepti knew who they were, and her heart fluttered with a thrill that they'd gotten away. They were gone as quickly as they came, and she explained to Larry who they were.

"I'll pick them up on the way out. They'll need a ride. Does that mean it's over?"

"I didn't see Isla."

"I couldn't see shit."

"Yeah, but I would have noticed her. You spend all that time locked up with someone, and you get to know them pretty well."

Bree stepped out from behind her tree. "Was that…?"

Deepti gave her theory again. "But no Isla."

The darkness in the trees offered Bree no answers. "And no Carter."

"Let's keep going," Deepti said.

Larry loosened his grip on her, only then realizing he'd been holding her the entire time. "You ever get scared?"

"Sure," she said. "Scared of not doing anything. Especially with these limp dick mother fuckers."

Larry had to smile. "Well, shit. Lead the way."

* * *

Ivana had one hand on the door handle, listening to the sound cascading through the trees. When she saw who was was coming at them, she let go. She stepped into the headlight glow and held up both hands to halt them. In Spanish, she told them they were safe.

A few dodged into the trees, but a few men and women stopped. Katie joined in, speaking Spanish and assuring them that they were being rescued. Neither woman looked like a threat, and both speaking Spanish meant something.

A man near the front called out to his colleagues who had hidden in the trees. In a minute, a circle formed, and tears were shed. Men and women hugged and then reached out for Ivana and Katie, who were pulled into the mass of bodies, all sharing the joy of being freed.

Carter couldn't hold it any longer. The movement, the tension in his body, the need for release meant he had to stop and set down the shotgun, unzip, and piss against a tree. He did so quickly because once the urge fell so intensely on him, he very nearly waited too long. The relief came with a burning and a cramp in his gut beyond what he'd been enduring, and getting used to, for the past few hours. Like a fuse burning down from his bladder through his urethra.

He'd moved to the front of the truck now, and the white light of the headlamps cast the trees in a soft moon glow that the fading red flare couldn't overpower. He tried to see if there was more blood, but it was too hard to make out against the dark of the tree bark.

After the last shot, the woods had gone fairly quiet. His focus held on his bladder and on the pain burrowed inside him like it was taking root. Not a temporary visit this time, a permanent resident. He didn't hear Luke step up behind him.

"Who the fuck are you?"

Carter lifted his hands. The shotgun lay useless by his feet.

"Can I zip up?"

"Go ahead."

Carter did and turned slowly. Luke stood silhouetted by the headlights in the distance, the gun held firmly in his hand.

"So who are you?"

"A friend of one of the people you abducted."

"This is government business," Luke said, clinging to his lie. He repeated the rote line he used on the missions, finally hearing how hollow it sounded. "We're authorized by the President of the United States to collect any suspected illegal immigrants and turn them over to detention for processing and deportation."

"Suspected isn't proven."

"You're an American," he said, taking on face value that Carter's white face and Midwestern accent made him somehow more American than someone like Ivana or Isla. "Don't you want to take back our country?"

"Take it back from who?"

"The illegal invasion."

"Son, you've been fed a plate of bullshit, and they tell you it's steak. This is a nation of immigrants. Your people came from somewhere. I don't know where, and I don't give a shit. But it's not up to you to judge who else is more American than you."

"The President authorized me to–"

"If you want to shoot me, go ahead. But I don't want the last thing I hear to be about that asshole."

Luke adjusted his grip on the gun. "Your friend is gone. They all ran away."

"Oh, I got her back at your house. I'm after one they call Isla." Carter inched his foot toward the shotgun. He calculated the probability of hooking his shoe under it and flipping it up to where he could catch it and fire, and knew immediately it couldn't be done. The pistol was much closer, but even that would be near impossible.

"What do you mean you already got her?"

"Ivana is my friend. She wasn't in your truck. I came out here to help get Isla back, too. And the rest of them." He began to ease his hands down, moving slow enough he hoped not to be noticed.

Luke shuffled his feet. "They hired some old man? What are you, some former special forces or Navy SEAL or something?"

"No, nothing like that. Just doing a favor. Hired means they would have paid me. I'm doing this for free." His hands dropped below his shoulders, easing down to where his pistol waited in his pocket.

"I don't fucking get you."

"I wouldn't expect you to. See, I give a shit about people. I realized I could help them, by getting rid of people like you."

Carter let his right hand dive into his pocket. He swiveled his hips, turning so he could get a clean shot. He crouched to get low, maybe duck under the shot he figured was coming from Luke's gun. As he pulled back on his arm, the gun snagged on the fabric of his pocket. The gun slipped from his hand, and his arm came away empty, then the gun spilled out the side and fell to the ground.

Luke took two steps forward and held the gun inches away from Carter's face. His pulse pounded fiercely until he could feel the blood pumping in his face. A simple pull of the trigger and the threat would be gone. One more body to the pile, it didn't matter now. Let them all run off into the woods, let this all slip away behind him. All Luke wanted was for this to be over, and he could go home. One slight tug of his index finger and it would be done. Luke let heavy breaths out of his mouth. The barrel of the gun trembled like a seismograph needle during an earthquake.

Carter's gut clenched, mocking his failed attempt at heroics. He repeated the same thing he'd been saying inside for months—one way or another, he was going soon. He bit down the pain and waited for the blast of the gun staring him in the eye. For as many times as he'd let himself wonder about it, this was not how he had imagined himself going out, but dying in the woods while trying to save someone was a hell of a lot better way to go than in a hospital bed.

Larry bent down and lifted a stick the size of a baseball bat off the ground. He and the girls all separated, putting a few trees between them all as they approached the clearing.

The flare had nearly burned down, and the light no longer reached the tops of the trees. The back of the truck lay open like a cave, the two bodies heaped on the ground below the opening. To the side, MJ's body lay flat, face down. He made no sound, no movement.

Bree looked over to Deepti, who gave a tiny shake of her head. Larry brought back the stick into a batter's position, wishing he'd brought something more powerful.

A high-pitched sound like a bird made all three snap their heads to the driver's side of the truck. Shuffling feet sounded from the shadow of the truck, then a shape appeared in the fading glow of the flare.

Isla. Behind her, Marco pushed her along. Her arm bent behind her, held by him to steer her to his will. A pistol pressed to her neck. She let out another tiny bird-like whimper.

"Just who the fuck are you people?" Marco said.

"Let her go," Deepti commanded with all the courage she could muster.

"Aw, fuck. It's you. Listen, you mouthy little bitch, you had your chance to run away. Why didn't you take it?"

"You watch how you talk to her," Larry said.

Marco tightened his grip on Isla and turned her toward Larry. "How about you take these bitches and go. This ain't your concern."

"You got that wrong, buddy."

Deepti took a step forward. "Let her go, you asshole. Can't you see this is over?"

"All I see is I got a gun, and you got a stick."

"We got a whole team of cops on their way up here. You're fucked."

"Bullshit."

Deepti took two more steps forward. "Try me."

"I've had enough of this." Marco pulled the gun away from Isla's neck. He turned it toward Deepti and fired. The sound boomed through the clearing like a cannon shot. Deepti grunted and fell to the ground.

Carter jerked at the shot, but it hadn't come from Luke's gun. Luke whipped his head around to look back toward the truck. Carter knew he could make a leap for the pistol aimed at him. He also knew he'd likely come up short. He had to try. He tensed and tried to will his muscles to push him forward, but the cramps in his gut held him in place.

Luke turned back. He lowered the gun.

"I didn't want to hurt anybody."

Carter knew better than to disagree or pile on right then. If Luke didn't see how his actions had hurt people beyond killing them, he might learn it in time. He let Luke live in his regret and his apparent change of heart.

"Who still has a gun out there?" Carter asked.

"Probably Marco."

"I need to go check that out. Are you gonna stop me?"

Luke stared at the old man. The headlights made Carter look pale, and being down on his knees made him small. "No."

Carter stood slowly, pausing twice to let the pain run through him like water draining away. He brought the shotgun with him, first using it like a cane to push himself up to a full stand. He had no reason to trust Luke, but he had every reason to try. He moved past him, angling for the truck and the clearing beyond. When his back faced Luke, he braced for a shot, but nothing came.

He nearly tripped over MJ's body as he stuck close to the side of the truck, starting out of sight. He could see Larry sprawled out over Deepti's body, shielding her from another shot. Bree stood close to a tree for shelter on the far side of the clearing. He couldn't see Marco, but he heard him when he began to shout.

"You take her and go in the next ten seconds, and I'll let you leave. After that, you made your choice."

"Don't shoot," Bree called out. She ran forward and joined Larry, hovered over Deepti.

Slowly emerging like a shark coming up from the deep, Marco stepped forward into the circle of dim flare light. He held Isla out in front of him, but his back faced Carter.

Larry still had ahold of the stick as he tried to cover as much of Deepti as he could with his bulk.

"Is she alive?" Bree asked.

"That motherfucker," Deepti growled. Bree had her answer.

"Let's go. Get her up."

Larry finally let go of the stick and got to his knees. "Can you stand?"

"I think so. Bastard shot me in my thigh."

"Better than most places," Larry said. He draped her arm around his shoulder and stood, pulling her with him. Bree slid under her other arm.

"Now get the hell out of here," Marco said.

"Let her go," Deepti said. "She's coming with us."

"Five seconds," Marco warned.

"I'm not leaving without her."

Larry faced Marco, the red making his face look like it had been painted. "Neither am I."

Bree joined in, "Me either."

Marco pressed the gun harder into Isla's neck. "Y'all are fuckin' stupid."

Carter stepped from the shadow of the truck. "Oh, I think you're the stupid one."

Marco pivoted to face the new voice joining the conversation. Isla twisted toward Carter and used the momentum from the spin to rotate her body and let her legs go slack. She slid from Marco's grip and fell to the forest floor, her arm sliding through his hand like the end of a rope holding him up from a deadly fall.

Carter took one step forward and fired the shotgun. The spray of pellets made tiny indents in his Kevlar vest, but the spread fanned wide and holes opened in the flesh of his neck, his cheeks, his forehead. A single pellet passed through his right eye with a tiny burst of fluid. Marco fell back. The blood that sprang from his neck was nearly invisible in the red light. Carter moved forward quickly, putting a foot on Marco's wrist so he couldn't lift his gun again. Isla clawed at the ground to pull herself away.

Marco looked up at Carter with one good eye as the old man loomed over him, his face a mask of shadow and red light.

Marco's breathing came ragged and shallow, the holes in his neck poking caverns in his throat. "I've been authorized by the President of the United States…" He drew a breath, then coughed. A spray of blood coated his lips and fell back onto his cheeks. "…by executive order…" Marco went slack. His breathing slowed.

"Everyone okay?" Carter asked.

"She's hit," Larry said. "In the leg."

"Get her back to the car."

"Is that all of them?" Bree asked.

A crunch of dry pine needles announced Luke as he stepped around the edge of the truck. He held his gun low against his leg, staring at Marco's prone body.

With a sound of rage that built in her chest and forced its way from her throat like an eruption, Isla dove forward, lifted MJ's gun off the ground by his body, and crouched to her knees, aiming at Luke.

Luke made no move to raise his gun.

"Wait, Isla! No!" Carter said. "Put it down."

He dropped the shotgun and crossed the clearing. Isla sobbed and shook, continuing to make primal sounds in her chest. Luke did nothing but stand there, waiting for the shot.

Carter reached her and put his hand over her wrist. He aimed the gun at the ground. "You don't want to do this. Come on. Drop it."

She let out a deep sob, barely catching her breath in time for another. She let her hand go slack, and Carter slipped the gun from her grip.

Luke let his gun fall to the ground.

Carter moved toward him. He stood a foot away, the gun low and pointed away.

"Go. Start walking."

Luke lifted his eyes to the old man, confused. Carter said it again, "Go."

Luke opened his mouth to speak, but stayed silent. Larry and Bree held Deepti up like soldiers on a battlefield as they moved past Marco's prone body and across the clearing. Luke took a small step forward to where Isla wept, her fingers dug into the dirt, looking like he might finally find words to say, but he stopped and let his mouth hang open. He met Carter's eye, recognized the chance he was being given, then turned and walked away into the shadows between the trees.

FIVE

Larry carried Deepti back to the car. He placed her on his lap in the front seat, holding pressure on her leg with the scrap of fabric he'd torn from his shirt.

Carter got back into his rental, and Chester greeted him with wet kisses and a low gruff.

"Yeah, I missed you too."

Isla climbed into the back seat of the rental.

"Let's get you home," he said. "I know your sister wants to see you."

At the mention of Marta, Island began to cry again. Carter started the engine and took a moment to let out a few deep breaths. His body ached all over, and he burned like he carried a fever. He thought for a moment that he should let Isla drive, but she was in worse shape than him so he drew in a sharp breath through his nose and put the car in gear. Chester leaned over the seat to sniff at Isla. She bent forward, put her head between her knees, and sobbed.

Ivana and Katie led the procession of escaped hostages down the road to the waiting semi trucks.

Carter followed Bree down the mountain as she sped to get Deepti to safety. They retraced the route down the mountain faster than they should have, Bree kicking up a cloud of dust behind her. Carter had to back off a little to get clear of it. They reached the flat ground with two waiting semi trucks.

Chuck met them on the road."Were those shots I heard?" Chuck asked. "Sounded like hunting season."

"Something like that," Carter said. He explained to Chuck about the people on their way down behind them. "We couldn't wait because we need to get her to a hospital."

"I can take them and drop them wherever they need to go," Chuck said.

"Thanks for all your help with this."

"If anyone asks, what should I tell them happened here?"

"You were never here. You don't know a damn thing."

Chuck nodded and went to the back of his rig to move some cargo and make space for passengers.

Larry stayed focused on getting Deepti into his truck. He set her in the seat and made sure she was comfortable as she could be.

"Let's get you to a hospital," he said.

"I can take her, really," Bree said.

"It's all right," Larry said. "I got it."

"We'll meet you there."

"You get her back home." He nodded his head at Isla. "We'll be okay."

Larry fired up his rig with a deep rumble.

"It's nice in here," Deepti said. "Roomy."

"Yeah, not so bad," Larry said, smiling at her.

Bree found Carter leaning on the bumper of Larry's truck, looking pale and weak. "Are you okay?" she asked.

"Yeah. I think so."

"It's over."

Carter nodded. "Yeah."

He knew he meant more than rescuing Isla. His time wielding a gun was over. His time helping people with violence. Maybe—likely even—his time on Earth.

The ball of heat in his gut hadn't subsided. A tiredness sank down to his bones.

"I'll go with Larry," he said. "You get Isla home to her sister. I'll see you at the apartment."

"You sure? I can stay with you."

"No, it's okay. You stay and help Ivana and Katie. They'll need it. They get everyone home."

She hugged him and went back to the car, passing Isla, who stopped and stood before Carter.

"Thank you."

"I didn't do much," Carter said. "You should be thanking Ivana. And those girls. They were really looking out for you."

"I know. But you don't even know me. You came all this way."

"I don't have to know someone to care if they're okay."

"Well, thank you anyway."

She walked back to Bree's car. Chuck called out from his truck, "Larry, I'll be in touch, man. We need to sit down over a drink and talk about all this." He laughed a high-pitched cackle.

Carter pushed himself off the bumper of Larry's truck. He looked up into the cab and waved. "I'll follow you." Larry gave him a thumbs up and executed a perfect three-point turn. Carter followed him back toward the highway.

Ten minutes later, Ivana, Katie, and the caravan emerged from the darkness. They were reluctant to get back into the cargo hold of a truck, but Chuck spoke a little Spanish and tried to reassure them. Ivana took each person by the hand and promised it would be okay. Once the truck was loaded, they followed the access road back toward the highway, leaving the mountain to the dark and the quiet again.

Somewhere up in the trees, far from any roads or trails, Luke worked to make his way down the hillside, hoping he would make it out alive to start a new life.

Once he parked at the hospital, he took Chester out for a break.

"I'll get you something to eat," he said.

He found the cafeteria and bought a double cheeseburger and a bottle of water, brought it back to the car, and let Chester chow down.

"I'll be back, buddy."

Inside, he found Larry in the ER waiting room.

"She's inside getting looked at," Larry said.

"Thanks for helping."

"Of course. That's one tough woman right there."

Carter smiled. "Do I detect something a little more than just respect?"

Larry looked at his shoes. "I mean, she's a handsome woman, no doubt. She wouldn't go for a road dog like me."

"Don't sell yourself short. You're showing her your heroic side."

"Maybe."

Carter found a water cooler. He filled a small paper cup. As he lifted it to drink, it slipped from his hand. A nurse passing by asked, "Is everything all right, sir? Did you need help?"

"No, no. Just clumsy. Sorry about that."

"It's okay. I'll get a porter." She studied him closer. "You sure you don't need to see anyone?"

"I'm okay. Just here with a friend."

Carter filled a new cup with water and walked back to the bench seats in the ER. A doctor came out and gave Larry the update. The prognosis sounded good.

"She'll have to stay in overnight for observation, but it was a clean exit. We should get the stitches all done in about an hour."

"Okay, thanks, Doc."

When they were alone again, Larry turned to Carter. "You can take off. I'll stay with her."

"Yeah, good call. Don't want to distract her with my handsomeness."

Larry held out a hand. "It's really been something meeting you, Carter McCoy."

"Likewise." They shook. "Sorry to drag you into all this, but I sure am glad you answered the call."

"My pleasure."

Carter stood to go, and a rush of dizziness came over him. The edges of his vision darkened, curtains drawing in. The world sped up and tilted too far on its axis, his brain inside a carnival ride. He reached out a hand to steady himself on a chair, but missed. He fell and blacked out before he hit the floor.

When he woke up, Bree was there leaning over him like an angel ready to take him away. He recognized the familiar blandness of a hospital room. Didn't matter what state he was in, Midwest, West Coast, or anywhere in between, they all looked the same.

"I thought that was it," he said.

"So did I."

He rolled his tongue around the inside of his mouth, trying to work up some moisture. "Chester?"

"I got him back at the apartment. Larry dug your keys out of your pocket. That rental car is a mess, by the way."

"Yeah. Might not get my cleaning deposit back."

Bree held a cup of water for him, and Carter sipped from a straw.

"What'd they say?"

Bree looked as if she had news she didn't want to tell. "Not much. Asked a lot of questions I didn't know answers for. Nobody seems to know what to do."

"Nothing *to* do," he said. "Nothing for them to do, anyway. Me, I still got a few things." He looked at his arm. No IV this time. Sticky patches with wires running from his chest. Monitors by his bedside with heart rate, oxygen levels, blood pressure.

"Help me get out of here," he said.

"This is becoming a habit."

"You know I don't want to die here."

She nodded. She lifted a bag with his clothes in it from the floor next to her. "Get dressed."

Over the next week, Isla had reunited with Marta and the two had tracked down their parents, who were on their way back from work downstate to see their girls. Larry had cancelled his latest trip and stayed behind with Deepti to cater to her while she was off her feet as her leg healed. Carter had been by to visit once and liked the way she smiled at Larry when he leapt up to go get her a refill on her water bottle or to make her a plate of sliced fruit.

"Is he taking good care of you?" Carter asked.

"Yeah. It's kinda freaking me out."

"He means well."

"I can see that."

Bree and Katie returned to work, and Ivana gave the impression of working her way into taking over the taco shop, and none of the employees minded a bit. Orlando hadn't asked questions about how Isla got rescued. After what he'd seen about Carter, he figured not knowing would be best.

After her first shift, Orlando stopped her as she wiped down a table.

"Good to have you back. I was worried you might not want to stay after—"

"It's good to do something normal. Hey, thanks for all your help."

"Of course. You know I'd do anything for you."

"Aw, you're sweet."

He faltered. Paused. Stared at his feet.

"I hope you don't mind," Orlando said, then he lifted his eyes to hers and forced himself to look at her until he finished. "But I wanted to see if you'd go to dinner with me. Not here. Someplace else. Like a...date."

"A date?"

"Yeah."

Katie pushed a lock of hair behind her ear. She smiled. "Yeah. Okay. We could try that."

"Yeah? Really?"

"Sure. I mean, since you asked so nicely." She smiled at him, and he blushed and turned away.

"Okay. Great."

* * *

Even as winter shortened the days and brought what the locals called a cold breeze in off the water, Carter visited the beach every day. If he came all this way, he might as well see the ocean. Carter walked Chester in the brightly painted sunsets and marveled at the even temperature that never seemed to vary.

After all this borrowed time, it still surprised him to get these extra days. His body had settled into an even rhythm that reminded him of the tide.

On Thursday of that week, when he finally felt up to it, he got Bree to drive him to a tattoo shop. He sat in a chair with a man named Grunt who inked a capital letter A on his wrist, with a shadow behind it. The lines were elegant, geometric. A symbol of Ava and Audrey in one simple image. Something he could take with him always, even into the dark.

He got a nod of respect from Grunt as he wiped antibiotic cream on the fresh tattoo and wrapped it in cling wrap. Carter didn't explain to him why the pain of the needle didn't bother him at all.

The pains in his gut had spread now. Getting out of bed took some time. His joints ached, and his head throbbed from the base, radiating pain down his spine. On Saturday, he went to the beach in the morning and sat in the sand with Chester by his side, and hadn't wanted to move for hours. The slow shushing of the waves calmed him. The soft pillow of sand cushioned his bones.

Bree came down after work in time for the sun to sink below the long stretches of clouds out over the water. She sat next to Carter as the clouds turned from white to orange and then pink, then a fiery red.

"I guess you're turning into a beach guy, huh?"

"Maybe. I can see the appeal."

Bree scratched Chester on his ears. "You thinking of heading back?"

"I don't know."

He stopped himself from saying all he had on his mind. It wasn't fair to burden Bree with that.

"Sorry if I got you into something dangerous," she said.

"I knew what I was getting into."

"I don't know how you don't get scared."

"Oh, I'm scared. Believe me, I'm plenty scared."

Carter picked up fists of sand and let it fall between his fingers.

"You want me to leave you alone?" Bree asked.

"No. Not yet. Stay with me a while." She leaned in and pressed her shoulder to his, and they watched the sun fall. Carter ran a finger over the tattooed A on his wrist. "No matter what you do, it always goes dark, I guess."

"Yeah. The world keeps turning," she said. "But then the sun rises, and we do it all again. I used to think I'd live my whole life in darkness, and now look at me. That's thanks to you."

"Ah, well…" He patted her hand. "One day I won't see the sun rise. But I want you to know, I don't regret any of it if you feel happy now. And if Ivana does, and Katie. And Isla."

"I'm happy. The others, too."

"Well, then I'm happy. Whether the sun comes up again or not."

She lifted her head, and he could see a tear in her eye threatening to fall. "Are you okay, Carter?"

"Look at the sun. When it gets closer to the horizon, it seems to speed up, doesn't it? Makes you realize how fast it's been traveling the whole time." The sting of salt in the air brought a tear to his own eye. He let it fall, feeling the cool line down his face as it caught a deeply etched line around his mouth. Chester grumbled and stretched himself out on the sand, lying his head on Carter's lap. "Chester has a home with you, right?"

"Of course."

"I'm glad you knew you could call me. It's too bad you never met Audrey. You two would have liked each other."

Bree leaned her head back on Carter's shoulder. They both stared out to sea as the sun dipped into the ocean as if it were diving under water. The bright orange ball disappeared, and the sky glowed with reflected light.

Carter went quiet. Bree's head spun with what to say, but none of it could ever be enough for everything she felt, or it sounded too saccharine, too Hallmark card. The sand under them contoured to their bodies, already cooling in the breeze coming off the water.

Even if they said nothing, everything between them was understood. Carter leaned into her, each holding the other up. His hand relaxed, and the last of the sand slid from his palm. She waited until a wave crashed, and in the pause between rushes of water, she said,

"I'm glad you came."

Acknowledgments

Big thanks to the team at Level Best Books. To my agent Wayne Arthurson and the team at The Rights Factory. Thanks to the voters at International Thriller Awards and the Anthony Awards who nominated Carter for prizes. To the readers who all agree that Chester is the best character I've ever written. To my wife and my girls for putting up with my side hustle.

About the Author

Eric Beetner has been hailed as "the new maestro of noir" by Ken Bruen and "The 21st Century's answer to Jim Thompson" by LitReactor. He has written more than 30 novels, and his 100+ short stories have been featured in over 35 anthologies. Along the way, he's been nominated for two ITW awards, a Shamus, a Derringer, and four Anthony awards. He's won none of them.

His novels include the Carter McCoy series, including the multiple award-nominated *The Last Few Miles of Road*, as well as *Rumrunners, The Devil Doesn't Want Me, There and Back,* and *All the Way Down.* For more, visit ericbeetner.com

AUTHOR WEBSITE:
www.ericbeetner.com

SOCIAL MEDIA HANDLES:
Facebook: EricBeetner

Instagram: @ericbeetner
Bluesky: @ericbeetner

Also by Eric Beetner

Standalone novels:
All The Way Down
There and Back
Two In The Head
Criminal Economics
The Year I Died 7 Times
Dig Two Graves
Nine Toes In The Grave
White Hot Pistol
Blood On Their Hands
Stripper Pole At The End Of The World

The Lars & Shaine series:
The Devil Doesn't Want Me
When The Devil Comes To Call
The Devil At Your Door

The McGraw series:
Rumrunners
Sideswipe
Leadfoot

The List series (with Frank Zafiro):
The Backlist
The Short List
The Getaway List
The Split List

With JB Kohl:
One Too Many Blows To The Head

Borrowed Trouble
Over Their Heads

Other series contributions:
  Blood & Tacos: Burritos & Bullets
  A Grifter's Song: The Sound Of Breaking Bones

Fightcard: Split Decision

Fightcard: A Mouth Full Of Blood

The Lawyer: Six Guns At Sundown

The Lawyer: Blood Moon

www.ingramcontent.com/pod-product-compliance
Lightning Source LLC
Chambersburg PA
CBHW060524160726